COURT OF SECRETS

Forbidden Queen Book One

DYAN CHICK

Illaria Publishing LLC

Published by Illaria Publishing LLC
Copyright © 2018 by Dyan Chick

Cover Artwork by Sanja Balan (Sanja's Covers)
Editing by Elizabeth A. Lance (EAL Editing Services)

Chapter One

❦

Nani hummed as she twisted my long blonde hair around the flowers and jewels she'd gathered for today. Occasionally, one of the other servants would say something to her and they'd chatter away, full of optimism for me, while clouds of dread floated around me, threatening to block all the light.

Knots twisted in my stomach, and I fought the urge to tell my maids to leave me alone so I could curl up in a little ball on my bed and cry for a while. If I thought I could get away with that in secret, I'd be tempted to try it. But as it was, half of the maids who were flitting in and out of my rooms were on loan to my family from my betrothed's household. How would he feel if they took word back that his bride-to-be wasn't thrilled to marry him today?

I stared at my reflection in the mirror mounted above my dressing table. Another gift from the wealthy Baron I was about to marry. Nani and the others were turning me into someone I hardly recognized. The jewels in my hair were worth more than my family made in a year and the whole thing seemed superfluous. It was all for show. They wanted me to look the part of a Baron's wife, rather than the daughter of a simple Knight. I knew my pretty face was the only reason this wedding was happening and the thought made me squirm in my chair.

"Cassia," Nani stopped working on my hair and rested her hands on my shoulders. "Today is a good day. You'll have an easy life and be cared for."

I managed a weak smile and set my hand on top of hers. How did I explain that I didn't want an easy life? I wanted adventure and excitement. I wanted freedom and wind blowing through my hair. How much of that would I get as a Baron's wife? I knew my future would be entertaining nobles and running a household that was too big. Then, when children came along, I'd have to manage their lives too. My days of riding my horse and climbing trees were over.

"You'll get used to it," Nani said, as if she could read my mind.

I sighed, knowing I couldn't keep anything from her. Nani had been my personal maid since as long as I could remember. Apparently, my mother had hired her after my sister was born to help care for me. She raised me, spending more time with me than either of my parents. I was going to miss her the most when I left this house.

"I don't want to get used to it," I said. "Why can't they marry Rose to the Baron? I'd be happy with a peasant."

"Hush, Cassia," Nani chided as she smoothed my curls with her gentle hands.

It was true, I didn't have the same ambitions as my family. My father was over the moon when he secured this marriage for me. It was a big step up in the social politics of the kingdom of Parlis. I wondered if things were different in any of our neighboring kingdoms?

My family barely counted as nobility since my father had earned his title in the last war with Udena, our neighbor to the south. It cost my family more than we made to keep up the facade of wealth, but my father was willing to do almost anything to play the game of courts and politics. I wanted nothing to do with any of it.

With a heavy sigh, Nani went back to fixing the curls on my head. By the end of the day today, I would be a Baroness and my father would get everything he ever dreamed. My marriage was his ticket to continue to climb the social ladder, his mind set on gaining favor with the king himself. Though, how a Baron was going to grant him that, I didn't know. Part of me wished my marriage was somewhere far away, in a different kingdom, where he would be less inclined to visit.

A gentle knock on the door broke me from my musings. The activity in the room halted at the sound and every pair of eyes turned to the door.

"Who is it?" I called.

"It's Rose," my sister called as she opened the door. She was wearing a grey dress that looked like it was made of liquid silver. The fabric pooled on the ground as she walked softly toward me. While my over the top expensive dress had been a gift from my future husband, I knew hers was paid for by our family. I didn't want to know what my parents had promised to obtain a dress of such quality.

I scowled at her, feeling heat rise to my cheeks at her presence alone. She was my older sister, yet she was dodging this marriage for reasons that were never explained to me, no matter how many times I insisted that the oldest daughter should be married first.

She liked to tell us she was interested in serving as a priestess in the Moon Temple, but I knew that was never going to happen. She was far too shallow to live a life of simplicity in a remote mountain maiden community. Her rouged cheeks and painted eyes were sign enough for me that her vanity was too great for that role.

I could have used that excuse myself and volunteered to join the maidens, but we all knew I valued my freedom too much. Though, a cloistered life of servitude to a goddess was probably not much different than the requirements of being a Baron's wife when it came to making my own choices. My best bet was that my husband would travel frequently, giving me the run of the home while he was away.

"What are you doing here, Rose?" I asked.

"Cassia," Nani scolded.

Rose glided over to me and one of the maids in my room brought her a chair. She sat down so she was across from me and stared at me with her large blue eyes. "Can't I come to wish my younger sister well before her wedding?"

The words came out as sweet as sugar, but I knew better. I wasn't sure exactly why she treated me as a rival, I certainly never wanted the same things that she did, but that was all I remembered of our childhood. Rose constantly trying to outdo me, making me feel inferior.

Fixing my best smile on my lips, I reached my hand out and set it on top of hers. My whole life, I'd dreamed of something greater than the manor we'd grown up in. So had Rose. Though I wanted adventure and new worlds, whereas she wanted riches and luxury. Despite the fact that we were so different, in the end, we both just wanted out. Away from our parents and on to better things. Who knew, I might even miss her when I was gone. "Thank you, dear sister."

Her lips twitched, her smile faltering for a fraction of a second. She was thrown off by my sudden kindness, but only for a moment. Quickly, she composed herself and clasped my offered hand in between her own. "I can't believe my little sister will be a woman today."

She leaned in, eyes sparkling with excitement. Gold curls fell in front of her face, but she ignored them. Looking at her was better than looking in a mirror. Everyone said we could have been twins. I think that was part of why she disliked having me around. If I'd been ugly, maybe she could have loved me.

4

"Are you prepared for tonight?" she whispered, as if she wanted to offer me advice.

"Lady Rose," Nani chided. "You shouldn't speak of such things."

Rose giggled, then let go of my hand. "I hear the first time hurts."

"It does, Lady Cassia, but it will not hurt long," Nani offered. "I'm all finished and you look like a queen."

Rose's lips twitched again and I smiled. Her discomfort was sign enough that Nani's skilled fingers had excelled once again. I had no doubt that I would look beautiful today with Nani's help.

"Here." Nani held up a silver hand mirror for me and I took it from her.

My eyes widened at the sight. She'd woven my long blonde hair into a crown on top of my head. Tiny wildflowers added hints of bright yellow and green. Jewels the color of champagne and berries added sparkle wherever the light touched.

At my request, she'd kept my face as my own, no added color to my lips or charcoal under my eyes. But she's dusted my cheeks with a fine powder that made my face shimmer in the light. "I look like a faerie."

"Hush now," Nani said, giving me a stern look.

I'd grown up on Nani's story about the faeries that lived in the other realm. It had been so long since anyone had seen them, that many people, including my sister, Rose, thought they were just a myth or at least extinct.

Whether or not they were real, I enjoyed the stories so much that the world had stuck with me. Immortal beings of immeasurable beauty who could control the elements sounded like an ideal way to escape. Rose, on the other hand had always fixated on the darker parts of the faerie stories that Nani told us.

Our parents didn't like the stories at all. They wanted us to be educated only in the things that would help us gain husbands and encouraged us to keep our heads away from daydreams. And here I was, on my wedding day, making all of their dreams come true.

Two of my maids carried over the gown that had been an early bridal gift from the family I was about to marry into. The collar was beaded and covered in jewels and beads and lace trimmed the waistline into the skirt below. The extra weight from the embellishments made it the heaviest thing I'd ever worn. The skirts were made of shimmering iridescent gold fabric that reminded me of the fabric on Rose's dress. I wondered if it was the same material, but I had never spent much time learning the names of fabrics.

As if reading my mind, Rose touched the bottom of my dress as my maids held it up for me. "This is excellent quality silk, Cassia." She stood, and smoothed the wrinkles out of her own dress. "Like mine."

Another girl might get angry with her own sister trying to upstage her on her wedding day. I wasn't that kind of girl. The only thing that bothered me about Rose's dress, was the amount of time it was going to take my family to pay for it.

I had a feeling the move was calculated, seen as an investment by our parents. I wondered how much of my own wedding was a trap set for unwed members of the Baron's social circle. It wouldn't surprise me at all if my marriage was a set up to help get a better husband for my sister. She was the oldest, after all, and would inherit our family's estate. The second child wasn't as important in the grand scheme of things. I tried to push these thoughts from my mind. I shouldn't care what my parents were plotting. I was about to be running my own household. At least I'd get my wish of getting away from here. Even if it wasn't exactly as I dreamed.

I carefully stepped into my wedding gown and my maids slid it up my body. The dress felt like water against my skin. It was so smooth and luxurious that even the extra weight of the fabric didn't bother me. Practiced fingers worked through all the buttons that went up the back of the dress until I was sealed up in the gown that was to bind me to one man for the rest of my days. I tried to ignore the tightness in my chest. Wasn't I supposed to be happy today?

The Baron wasn't an unattractive man. He seemed nice enough, but the closer we got, the more I felt like a wolf who'd been broken to act like a dog. In some ways, I wondered why I wasn't more like Rose. I never quite fit in, which made it harder for me. Things would be easier if I just accepted it or got excited about it like a girl my age was supposed to do.

I turned, and the skirts of my gown moved with me in a whisper of swirling threads. I had to admit, it was stunning. I ran my fingers over the details in the bodice and down to the flowing fabric at my waist and took a deep breath. Wearing this made everything feel so real. This was actually happening. Perhaps I could convince myself that everything would be alright in the end.

Nani set her hands on my shoulder and pressed her cheek against mine. "You look beautiful, like the autumn sunrise. I've never been so proud of you in all my life."

The words were sweet, but it hurt a little at how much everyone was getting worked up about today. My only jobs were to look pretty, smile, and say the words at the wedding ceremony. To me, I wasn't doing anything grand or significant, unless you took into account the alliance and financial benefits this would bring to my family. I managed a weak smile, and nodded.

Nani gave me a small hug, clearly trying to avoid ruining my hair or wrinkling my dress. She backed away and stared lovingly at my face. I wondered if she was memorizing what I looked like. I was doing the same thing, wondering what life would be like without her telling me what to do and helping me with every aspect of my day. She would stay here, to remain in my parents' household, while I was surrounded by strangers starting tomorrow. That was the one thing I had requested in all of this, to spend the wedding night in my own home.

It was tradition to have the wedding at the bride's home, so some households allowed their daughter one more night in her childhood bed. Other families insisted that the bride and groom be swept away to his home that very evening.

Since the Baron's estate was nearly a full day's ride by horseback, I was granted the evening to rest here in my home. I wasn't sure if the Baron would feel comfortable coming into my room tonight. I hoped he wouldn't, even though I knew once the ceremony was complete, it would be his right as my husband. The whole thing made my stomach twist into knots again. If only there were something I could do that didn't involve living on a secluded mountaintop surrounded by other women for the rest of my existence.

Another knock on the door caused all the chatter in the room to cease. Blood thrummed in my ears and I held my breath for a moment as the doorknob turned. I knew it had to be time.

My mother stood framed by the door, her face solemn. She wore a dress of deep blue trimmed in ivory, our house colors. Her once golden hair, now streaked with gray, was intricately woven into a braid on top of her head. She looked stunning, an older version of my sister and myself.

She took a few steps into the room and stopped in front of me, clasping her hands at her waist. "You look beautiful, Cassia. You will make your family proud today."

"Thank you, Mother." My tongue felt dry, as if I'd swallowed sand.

She offered her arm and I took it, letting her lead me to the gathered crowd waiting in our gardens. By sunset, I would be a Baroness and I felt like a flame burning within me was being snuffed out.

Chapter Two

❦

"You could appear more cheerful," my mother said as we walked from my room toward the grand staircase.

With one arm looped through my mother's elbow, I held my dress up with my other hand to prevent stepping on it as we descended the stairway. I turned to my mother and smiled. My stomach was still too nervous to form any coherent words.

At the bottom of the stairs my father waited for us. He wore a velvet tunic and I could see the perspiration shining on his face. Medals were hung on his chest and he wore the red sash of the royal knights.

My family had come from a long line of merchants, some of the wealthiest in the land. The comfort provided by several generations of successful business wasn't enough for my father. He had to have the status that went with it even if it cost him multiple generations of his family's hard earned wealth to reach it.

"Darling," my father offered his hand to me, palm up, and I set my fingers tentatively in his grasp. "You look beautiful."

I curtsied, and moved forward, allowing him to lead me to the front door. "Thank you, Father."

"I know this isn't what you want to be doing. I know how much you value your freedom. And that's my fault, I was too lenient as a father."

"That's not true," I objected.

My father held up his hand indicating that he wanted me to stop talking. I clamped my mouth shut.

"Since I was away for most of your youth, you were given time to do things that most young ladies don't. All of the time spent in the fields riding your horse without a chaperone present, all of that interacting with peasants and farmhands."

"They were my friends," I said. The wound was still fresh, even though it had been over a year since my father had forbade me from speaking with any of the people that were below us in his newly acquired rank. I had disobeyed a few times, but my father knew too well that if he punished me, I would only continue to disobey. Instead, he threatened those around us for violating his rule. After that, none of my childhood playmates were willing to risk spending any time with me.

"I know you think I've been tough on you, Cassia." My father turned my chin so I was forced to look him in the eye. "But I do care for you, in the best way I can. And that is why I have come to an arrangement with your soon-to-be husband."

I straightened, the tiniest flicker of hope trying to break through the unease I felt. "What kind of arrangement?"

"You will be permitted to continue your riding," my father said. "Without a chaperone once you have grown accustomed to your new home. It took some negotiation on my part, but I was able to convince him that if he wants a happy wife, allowing you a taste of freedom on occasion would be in his best interest."

Coming from my father, this was the best gift he could ever give. I let go of his hand and gave him a hug. The kind of hug I hadn't given him in years, not since I was a small child. He wasn't used to physical affection, and at first he tensed at the touch. But then his shoulders relaxed and he reached one arm around me and patted me gently on the back. That was about as good as it got from him.

I let go of my father and stepped back, lifting my chin higher. If I could be given time alone, away from the confines of daily life, just a little taste of freedom every now and then, maybe I would be able to survive this marriage. I might even find my own peace there.

"He's a good man," my father added. "He won't hurt you. Please, try to make him a little happy."

My cheeks flushed and I hoped my father wasn't referring to the same thing that my sister had referred to earlier today. But there was no way I was going to ask him for clarification. Instead, I took his hand again and took a deep breath.

"Are you ready?" he asked.

"Yes," I said, feigning confidence.

My father nodded to the servants stationed on either side of the doors. The men stepped forward, and opened them wide so that both of us could pass through the doors together.

Soft late afternoon sunshine filtered past the doors, illuminating the entryway. In front of us, the entire world was covered in a warm, golden glow.

It was a spectacular late summer day and no bride could have hoped for a better evening to celebrate her wedding. I licked my lips in anticipation and ignored my racing heart as my father guided me out of our house onto our manicured lawn.

Rose petals lined our way, trimmed with boughs of pine tied with gold ribbons to form a walkway. The smell was intoxicating, filling the air with the last remains of summer intermingling with the first taste of autumn.

I didn't plan a single detail for my wedding, but this was exactly what I would have chosen. A rush of gratitude surged through me as I considered the fact as much as I wanted to get away from them, and as much as I often disliked my sister, she and my mother had worked together to create something beautiful for me.

With each step, the gathered crowd drew nearer and I could hear my heart pounding in my ears. After three more heartbeats, heads started to turn toward us, as a low murmur sounded in the distance. Then the crowd stood in anticipation of our arrival.

The path of rose petals cut an aisle through the crowd that led to my fate. I let my body take over, allowing my mind to detach from the moment. If I overthought this, I might not make it through. But this was my future, this was for my family, and this was better than I could hope for as the youngest daughter. I should be grateful. I tried to be grateful.

As we walked between the waiting visitors, I felt like I wasn't even there. Like I was watching a stranger walk to her waiting groom. Ahead, I saw an archway that had been erected for us. The wooden frame woven with pine and roses, matching the path I'd just taken. A man stood under the archway, waiting for me. He was a stranger and this was the first time I'd seen him up close. The day my father and he met to agree on my marriage, I'd watched from my bedroom window as he exited our home. He'd turned and looked at me for a second, giving me a chance to see his face, before climbing atop his steed.

I studied his face and realized he was younger than I'd originally thought. He was clean shaven, with a shadow of dark hair that was already trying to grow back over a strong jaw. His skin was tanned from the sun and he had deep brown eyes. Straight black hair was pulled into a tail at the base of his head. He was a handsome man, and likely less than ten years older than me. I should consider myself lucky. Perhaps, being married to him wasn't going to be so bad.

We stopped in front of the waiting Baron and the high priest who was here to bind us under the eyes of the gods. My father kissed my cheek before passing my hand to the stranger who would be my husband for eternity. There were no second chances on marriage. This was my one chance. My chest constricted again and I took shallow breaths as my betrothed guided me to my place under the archway.

"Breathe, Cassia," he whispered as he flashed a smile. "I'm just as nervous as you. Just think of me as Aaron, ignore the titles, I'm no different than you."

His words made me relax, just a little, and I managed an actual smile as I took my place next to him.

The priest lifted his hands, indicating the start of the ceremony and I heard the rustle of fabric and creaking of chairs as the guests took their seats.

The next several minutes flew by as a priest completed the ceremony by setting a pair of matching floral wreaths on our heads. We turned toward each other in preparation for saying the words of commitment. My mouth was dry, my palms were sweaty as the priest set my hands into those of the man who would be my husband as soon as we said our words.

The Baron stared into my eyes and I realized he looked just as timid as I felt. This was new to him, too. We might be strangers, but perhaps this wouldn't be so bad after all.

He opened his mouth to speak, but I couldn't hear the words as a roar broke through the gardens. My ears rang, and I feared I was losing my mind. Then, I realized the sound wasn't in my head. It wasn't my own fear taking over.

The Baron dropped my hands and turned away from me. I followed his gaze and froze in fear at the sight in front of us.

Behind me, I could hear screams from our guests and mass commotion of tipping chairs and running people competed against another roar from the creature standing in front of us. I couldn't tear my eyes away from the beast, it was unlike anything I had ever seen before.

Hovering above us, flapping large leathery wings, the monster most closely resembled an overgrown bat that gained the ability to walk upright. It had leathery skin with splotches of fur in places it didn't belong. It had a snout that protruded from its face filled with large, pointed teeth. Drool dribbled down its jaw onto its hairy chest. Yellow eyes fixed on me and it tossed its head back before releasing another roar.

Next to me, the Baron was the first to regain control of his functions. He took off running, followed by the priest. I stood alone, still frozen in terror as I stared down the creature in front of me. It spread wide, leathery wings in front of me. They were lined with veins and nearly transparent. Then, the creature dropped to the ground, landing on all fours, wings still spread wide as it scurried toward me.

"Cassia!"

I turned my head to see Rose calling for me. She was waving frantically trying to get my attention.

"Cassia, run!"

I glanced back at the approaching beast, to find that it was no longer focused on me. Instead, it had turned its gaze upon my sister. It lunged forward taking wide steps made longer by gliding on its massive wings. Snapping its jaws, the beast headed right for my sister.

Something inside me clawed at my skin, as if trying to get out. It was as if I had my own beast that wouldn't stand for this. My sister might drive me crazy most of the time, but she was the only one I had. Fire roared to life within me and without thinking, I chased after the monster.

Somehow, I was able to reach my sister before the creature did and I shoved her out of the way, taking her place.

The beast reared when it approached me, rising up to its full height. Clawed forearms reached for me slashing through the air. I ducked away from them but not in time to prevent damage. The beast managed to grab my side, dragging its claws through my beautiful gown tearing a split right down the side. It was a wonder it didn't break the skin.

I glanced over at my sister to see her crawling away from the creature. No one else was around, everyone had fled. None of the knights, none of the merchants, none of the brave hunters had stayed to face off against this creature. I was on my own.

Chapter Three

Ｉ knew I couldn't fight off the creature like this by myself, but I wasn't sure I'd be able to run from it either. There weren't exactly any weapons around at a wedding, and it wasn't as if I would know how to use them anyway.

Before I could come up with a reasonable plan, the beast charged me. Instinct took over and I ran through the chairs, dodging and weaving through the leftover chaos of the fleeing guests. I heard the snarling of the creature as it chased me, drawing closer with each beat of my heart.

My legs burned from exertion and I pumped my arms as hard as I could trying to stay even one step ahead of those massive teeth. Confused, and terrified, I turned away from my home and two things flashed through my mind at that second. One, going opposite from all the others might draw the creature away from harming them. Two, if I could make it to the woods maybe I could hide.

I certainly knew climbing a tree wasn't going to help me defeat a creature that had wings, but there was enough under-growth and brush and winding paths in that forest that it wasn't unheard of for hunters to go in and never come out. It was part of why I had never been in the woods myself. The other reason was that Nani swore the woods would lead us straight to the Faerie Realm. As much as my father said it was nonsense, it would explain why so many seasoned hunters would randomly go missing. At this point, I was willing to take my chances.

I was seconds away from reaching the tree line, my only hope at survival. When suddenly, I noticed someone or something causing a lot of commotion in the trees ahead. Just as I passed into the trees I was knocked to the ground by a group of men coming out of the trees.

I landed face first in the dirt and by the time I rolled myself to all fours to see what was going on, the men who had nearly trampled me were chasing down the monster.

Feeling foolish, I righted myself and brushed the twigs and dirt from my dress as best I could. The gown was shredded, most of the beads from the bodice were missing, leaving dangling thread as the only sign of what had once been exquisite craftsmanship.

Panting, I took a few cautious steps away from the tree line back toward my family's land to see if I could catch a glimpse of what was happening with the beast.

For a moment, all was quiet, no sign of whoever it was that had come running out of the woods or the monster I had been fleeing from. I could hear the thumping of my own heart as I worked to slow my breathing and checked my surroundings. The hair on my arms stood on edge in anticipation as I half expected the creature to snap its jaws behind me at any second.

It took another few heartbeats for me to realize that this was my chance to run home, to join the others barricaded inside my family's manor, safely tucked away behind a locked door. Picking up the shredded remains of my skirt I wrapped the fabric around my arm near my waist so I would have more freedom to run. I took off, not bothering to look behind me, pumping my arms and legs as fast as I could, ignoring the searing pain in my lungs.

I could see the house in the distance, I could make it if I just kept going. Once again, I wove around the fallen chairs from the abandoned wedding ceremony. I jumped over broken items and dodged the scattered remains of my wedding day. One of my shoes flew off as I jumped and I doubled back to retrieve it, which turned out to be a mistake.

The beast was back, staring me down eye to eye. I could smell its putrid breath, and watched in horror as blood dribbled down its snout into the matted brown fur of its chest. I realized there was a familiarity to that stench. It was the smell of rotting, decaying meat. I wasn't sure what this creature had been eating, but I didn't want to be the next on the menu.

Trying not to break eye contact, I slowly backed away, hoping I could get some distance between us before I turned my back on it. The creature growled low in its throat, a warning sound. I froze, continuing to look in its eyes. If I stayed still it didn't seem to have any issue with me. So I waited, trying not to breathe in the smell through my nose.

Where had everybody gone? I had hoped by this time, my father and some of the other knights who had been invited to the wedding would have returned with weapons. Clearly, this beast would be an excellent trophy for any hunter. Why were they taking so long?

Slowly, I took another backward step and again the beast growled. I couldn't wait here all day, waiting for it to devour me. With one deep breath, I pivoted and took off again, hoping the creature wouldn't follow. I only got a few steps away before I was knocked to the ground.

I could feel the heat of the beast's breath on the back of my neck and I squeezed my eyes shut, not wanting to see those fangs as they bit into me. I gasped as a leg or arm or something pinned me to the ground, making it difficult to breathe.

Suddenly, the beast howled and I felt the pressure release from my back. I rolled over, to find the monster rearing on its hind legs, howling in pain. Using the opportunity to run for my life again, I rolled away from the creature and made it to my hands and knees before an arrow flew over my head and landed in the side of the monster, causing it to cry out in agony again.

I dropped to my stomach, not wanting to get hit by one of the flying arrows as it sought its target. Three more flew over my head hitting the beast in staccato succession. This time there was no cry of protest from the creature, only the sound of the beast hitting the ground. I lifted my head to look at the fallen creature and before I could bring myself to standing, it grabbed me. The long talon-like claws dug into my side as it dragged me over to it.

The creature held on to me as if I could shield it from any more damage. I screamed as pain splintered through my body from those claws. It spread through me like fire shooting through my veins.

The monster pulled me on top of it, and once again I found myself face-to-face with the terrible fangs. I turned away from the stinking breath, and the monster snapped its jaws at me. I didn't want to die and I tried to squirm away from its grasp, but the movement only made the claws dig further into my flesh.

I screamed again and used my arm to brace myself against the sweaty, matted fur. My hand brushed against one of the arrows that had impaled the falling creature. I yanked it out causing it to roar again, sending slime and saliva all over my face.

I gagged, bile rising to my throat, but fought it back, swallowing it down. Grasping the arrow in my hands I used every ounce of strength I had to lift that arrow above the creature's neck and thrust it into the soft skin under its powerful jaw.

The creature's eyes widened and blood sprayed from the wound and dribbled from its open jaw. I turned away, shielding my eyes as best I could as the warm liquid covered me. With one last contraction the beast drew me nearer to it until my nose was touching its snout.

It took everything I had not to vomit all over the stinking

beast. Then the creature shuddered, driving its claws deep into me. My insides felt like they were on fire. Searing heat shot through me, filling every inch of me with an explosion of pain that I feared might turn me inside out.

I cried out, fighting against the invading feeling. The beast's legs fell limp causing me to roll off of its gray body onto the ground, claws still impaled in my side. I wanted to cry again, but all I could do was whimper as tears streamed down my face.

My breathing was shallow, and I was worried that this was it. I was going to die right here with the claws of the stinking, horrible creature still in my side.

Using the last bit of energy I had, I tugged on the paw, yanking it away from me. A fresh wave of pain screamed through me as the claws tore out of my skin. Blood bloomed on my beautiful gown turning most of the bodice crimson within seconds. The world spun and I swore I saw two men looking down at me, but I wasn't certain of anything anymore. I felt like I was floating, and the pain eased as everything went black.

Chapter Four

Somewhere far away I could hear the sound of people talking. It sounded like my father and my mother and I thought I even heard Rose in the background. Everything hurt and I wanted to open my eyes to make sure I was still here, to make sure my body was there, but it hurt too much. So I let myself slip back into sleep.

I woke to the feeling of someone touching my side. I waited for the pain to crash in around me, but it didn't come.

"Cassia?" A woman's voice floated around my head.

It still wasn't clear where I was or what was happening.

"Cassia, can you hear me?"

I took deep breaths in and out. I didn't hurt anymore and fear seized me. Shouldn't I be in pain? Hadn't something terrible happened to me? I couldn't remember the details, but I knew the absence of pain was worrisome. Was I dead?

It all came flooding back in an instant, the wedding, and the attack by a giant beast creature with expansive bat like wings. Two male faces I didn't recognize floated before me then vanished into mist just as quickly as they had arrived. A memory of searing pain made me clench my side and then the pain was gone.

"Cassia, open your eyes," Nani's voice said.

I was sure it was her now, though I wasn't sure if I was really here. Perhaps this was just a dream, perhaps this was the underworld. There was only one way to find out.

Hesitantly, I opened my eyes and bright light momentarily blinded me. I lifted a hand to shield my face from the sunshine pouring in through my bedroom window.

Then it hit me, I was in my bedroom, where I belonged, with Nani. Did that mean that the attack had been a nightmare? Perhaps today was my wedding day and I was nervous about what was going to happen.

I sat up quickly and instantly regretted the decision as stars danced in front of my vision and my head spun. I lay back down and looked at Nani who was sitting vigil on my bed. "What happened?" I asked.

"There was an attack, dear child," she said. "It's a miracle you survived."

I reached for my side to feel the place where the claws dug into my flesh. The pain was gone, which made no sense. Claws like that should have killed me. I wondered if infection had set in and was giving me delusions. Or perhaps they had just given me so much syrup of the poppy that I couldn't feel a thing anymore.

Slowly I lifted up the white night shirt I'd been dressed in and looked down at my waist. Raised pink scars stretched from my bellybutton all the way around my waist to my back. The scars were a clear indication that those claws had not been in my imagination. "How long have I been out?"

The bigger question was how I managed to survive, but I wasn't sure I wanted to know the answer to that one. Something in the back of my mind was clawing at my memories as if trying to reveal something I should already know. Another part of me seemed to be actively repressing whatever it was that was trying to surface, which wasn't a good sign. Perhaps I blacked out all of the horrors they must've put my body through to heal that much damage. It must have been weeks of pain for the scars to have covered the open wounds.

"You can't stay here, child," Nani said.

That was the last thing I expected to hear from her. "What are you talking about?"

Nani's brow furrowed and her watery gray eyes were laced with concern. I wondered if she had even left my bed since the accident occurred.

"It's only been one night since the attack," Nani said.

"That's not possible," I said tracing my fingers over the scars. "Those claws should've killed me, not healed in hours."

I'd seen enough injuries in my lifetime to know what an open wound this size meant. Infection should have set in, that is, if I hadn't died from the blood loss first. There was no reason for me to still be alive. And there was no explaining how this had healed up on its own so quickly.

"I cleaned you up and I've kept your family away so far, but it's only a matter of time before they come in with the doctor to check your progress." Nani leaned forward and brushed my hair away from my face. "If they find you like this there's going to be questions and they won't like the answers."

"What kind of medicine did you find?" I asked the only thing that made sense in my head. Whatever Nani had done, it must have cost a fortune.

"I'm afraid it's not that simple. Medicine didn't heal you, you healed yourself."

"That's impossible," I said, tracing my fingers over the pink ribbons on my waist.

A quiet knock sounded on my door. Nani's eyes widened and the color drained from her face. She tugged my shirt down over the injury. "Pretend you're asleep," she whispered before pulling the covers up over me.

I had no reason to doubt Nani, so I did as she said, and closed my eyes and slowed my breathing so that I appeared to be sleeping.

"How is she?" my father asked.

"I stopped the bleeding but she'll need to rest more," Nani said. "I'll keep watch over her and let you know as soon as she wakes."

"Thank you, Nani. The physician will be here to check on her in a few hours. When he gets here, you can go get some rest." My father's boot steps leading away from the room let me know that he was no longer standing by the door. I heard the sound of the latch click as Nani must have closed the door behind him.

"Cassia," Nani said, settling back down on my bed. "Listen very carefully, child."

I opened my eyes and looked up at her. I hadn't seen an expression this grim or this serious on Nani's face since she had to tell me that a childhood friend had died of fever when I was seven. I couldn't imagine what she was about to say now.

"You're different, Cassia. There's a reason that you've never felt like you fit in here. Because you don't, you never belonged here. The stories I told you weren't stories, they were your history." Nani's shoulders sank. "I hoped I'd never have to tell you any of this."

I narrowed my eyes and furrowed my brow as I blinked up at Nani's worried expression. "I don't understand what you're saying."

"There's one story I never told you, because it's your story. When a Fae child is placed in a human home to be raised by humans, we call that child a changeling. They are rare in our world, and are only done in extreme circumstances. Changelings are stripped of their magic and raised as humans. After they've been here for twenty years, they lose their magic permanently. Most of the time, they never even realize they are not of this world. But now that you've come in contact with magic, I fear it has woken the magic buried inside."

My brow furrowed as her words sank in. I would be twenty in a few months, but I couldn't wrap my mind around what she was saying. Would I have never noticed this?

"Cassia, you're a changeling. You aren't human," she said.

"How can that be? You always told me the stories weren't real," I said.

The part of my mind that had been clawing to gain its freedom since I woke started to tingle as if reminding me that I never really thought they were just stories. Part of me always hoped that even though no one had seen the Fae for generations, there was some truth to her stories. Now that I was hearing Nani tell me it was all real, it didn't seem possible.

"My parents."

"Your mother gave birth to a baby girl who did not survive her first night. On that same day, you were born in faerie. I was charged with taking you to the human temple. When the midwife who delivered your mother's stillborn babe brought her for a blessing, I convinced her to return to the home with you. She told your mother that the fresh air and walk to the temple was enough to revive you."

I shook my head, not sure what I should believe. "I can't be fae. Look at my mother, at Rose. I look just like them."

Nani nodded. "You do. While most of your magic is dormant, changelings adapt to their surroundings. You grew to look like the human women around you and in turn, they grew to look more like you."

"That doesn't seem possible." Nani had been by my side as long as I could remember and she had no reason to lie to me. I lifted the nightshirt again and glanced at the scars. Something happened to heal those wounds. "If I were Fae," I said the words slowly, still not believing them, "what would that make you?"

"I am a brownie, a helper faerie. I served your Fae mother. Now, I serve you," she said.

"That doesn't make any sense," I said. "And even if I believed it, it doesn't explain why I'd need to leave here. Nobody else would ever believe I wasn't human."

"Those who do believe, might try to hurt you. That creature that attacked you wasn't from this world. It's from a place far more sinister. Something must have changed, something's not right in Faerie. You have no way of protecting yourself. You don't even know how to use your magic. I think it's time for you to return."

"Magic?" Now I was starting to doubt everything Nani said. I wanted to believe there were faeries somewhere beyond the trees, but it was difficult to wrap my mind around having magic of my own.

It was one of the things I loved about the faerie stories I heard growing up, and as much as I wished I could be something more than what I was, I couldn't find it in me to believe that I had magic in any form.

Nani lifted the nightshirt just enough to show the edge of the scars across my midsection. "How do you think those healed so quickly? Wounds like that should not heal in one night. And when they see that the damage is gone, they're going to accuse you of worse things than being Fae."

"How could they? My own family?" I wanted to believe that they would support me and defend me and be happy that I was healed. But I knew that wasn't true. My own father auctioned me off to the highest bidder and was more concerned about his status than anything else. If I were a threat to his reputation, he'd find a way to eliminate me.

A lump rose in my throat as I thought back to the day my father made me watch him end my favorite horse's life. She was old, and starting to have difficulty getting around. Rather than let me care for her like I wanted to, my father put a knife to her throat, telling me it was a great kindness to allow her to go quickly to death. I cried for hours, hating my father for what he had done. He never even showed a flicker of remorse. Would he do that to me? It wouldn't be difficult to tell everyone I had died from injuries sustained on my wedding day. Would he prefer that over having a daughter accused of witchcraft? Fear trickled down my spine like icy fingers. I knew Nani was right, even though I didn't want to believe it. "What do I do?"

"You have to flee, to the woods. Try to find the way in."

"How will I find it?" I asked. "And what if they don't let me in? Whoever left me here clearly didn't want me."

"Cassia, there are things you don't know," Nani said.

The door swung open and my father walked into the room, the doctor trailing behind him. My palms were sweaty and I looked up at Nani as dread seeped through me.

"You're awake," my father said, without a touch of happiness in his voice.

He was just making an observation. It didn't seem to matter to him if I was awake or not. Then, I decided that wasn't entirely true. To my father, I represented a substantial investment in his business. If anything happened to me, he couldn't marry me off.

"You may go," the doctor said to Nani.

I frowned, disliking the way the doctor so easily dismissed the most important person in my life. To everyone else, she was just a servant. To me, she was more my family than any of the others in this house. But in light of the revelation from Nani, it was possible there wasn't even blood to connect me to them. If she was telling the truth, I didn't have any family here.

Suddenly, I felt like I was surrounded by strangers, my head spun with the realization. I held my breath as the doctor approached, unsure of what I should do. I slammed my arm down on my side keeping my nightshirt in place. "It's feeling better, doctor. Please, don't touch it."

"Don't be foolish, girl." The doctor sat on the edge of my bed and moved my arm out of the way. "I'll be gentle, child," he said as he pulled the nightshirt up and as soon as he saw the healed flesh, his expression hardened.

"You said this was a fresh wound, why did you call me in for an old injury?" The Doctor stood and turned to my father. "My time is valuable, I cannot waste it on hysterical women. You need to get your daughter under control. If she were attacked by an animal, there would be injuries present." The doctor shook his head and pushed past my father as he stormed out of the room.

My heart raced as I waited to see how my father was going to react. His face was blank, unreadable. He reminded me of the quiet turn birds took right before a thunderstorm. Slowly, he walked over to me and looked at the scars on my side.

He scowled and shook his head. "I should send you away for this." He lifted his arm and I tensed, waiting for him to hit me. Instead, the back of his hand slammed into Nani's face. He grabbed her by her collar and dragged her away from the room. "I always suspected there was something unnatural about you."

I screamed, "Father, no!"

He paused at the doorway still holding onto Nani's collar.

She didn't put up a fight, and held her chin high. "It's alright, Cassia."

"No, no it's not alright," I said through the tears.

"This does not concern you, Cassia. We have laws here, magic is illegal," my father said.

"No, she didn't use magic," I said.

Nani smiled weakly. "Remember what I said."

My father dragged her from the room, then slammed the door behind them.

I swung my legs off the edge of the bed and tried to stand, but I was so weak that my body gave out from under me. I sat there, crumpled on the ground, as tears streamed down my face. I called after them, but my father and Nani were gone.

Chapter Five

If Nani was telling the truth, I was a magical creature, an immortal being. But if that were true, why did I feel so broken? It took every ounce of my energy to haul myself back up onto the edge of my bed.

My hands were shaking and I felt like I was recovering from an illness. Was she crazy? None of it seemed possible at all. As much as I would like to find out that I had some sort of power or something that may be special, it just didn't make sense.

It was true that I never felt like I belonged, never felt like I fit in, but I was sure lots of people felt that way. Especially girls forced into marriages that they didn't want.

Before I could figure out what I should do next, my door swung open and Rose appeared in my doorway. She walked into my room and stopped just short of where I sat on my bed. Hands on her hips she looked down at me, lips pulled together in a tight line. After several seconds, she finally dropped her arms. "Is it true?"

"Is what true?" I spat.

"That Nani's used magic to heal you." Lines from tears were still visible on Rose's face.

I was surprised to see an emotional response. I never thought she cared all that much about Nani, but then again, I wasn't sure Rose was capable of caring. Our parents tried to send all emotions away from both of us. I was never great at hiding mine to my father's despair.

Rose looked shaken and I couldn't tell if it was because she was afraid for Nani or she was worried about me. Either would surprise me, but given the expression on her face, either was possible.

"I don't know what happened." It was the truth, and that was all I knew. I didn't know what was happening. I didn't know what was going on. I wasn't sure if I should try and call after Nani or if I should be afraid of her. I didn't want to be afraid of her, there was nothing inside me telling me I should be afraid of her, but I couldn't explain anything that was happening to me.

"But the wounds, the injury, it's healed?" Rose asked.

I lifted my shirt showing her the scars.

Rose stumbled forward and collapsed on the bed next to me, covering the gasp that came out of her mouth with her hand. Tentatively, she reached her fingers out and brushed them against the raised scars. Then she shook her head, and dropped her hands to her lap. "I wouldn't have believed it if I hadn't seen it myself."

"Rose, where did Father take Nani?" I was afraid to hear the answer, but I needed to figure out what I was going to do next. And until I knew what they were doing with the woman who had raised me, crazy or not, I wouldn't be able to come up with a plan.

"I'm not sure," Rose said. "But Father has responsibilities, if he goes easy on her, it will make him look weak."

"And is it so wrong? Is it such a bad thing if it results in saving someone's life?" I asked.

Rose stood and walked toward the door pivoting back to look at me when she reached it. "For your sake, I won't tell anyone what you just said." Then she left my room.

I forced myself to stand and walked on shaky legs over to

where my dressing gown was hanging on a hook on the wall. The simple act of pulling the sleeves on and tying the belt around my waist was exhausting enough that I had to sit for a moment to catch my breath again.

While I waited, I heard the movements of another visitor outside my door. Rose hadn't bothered to close it behind her. Whoever was approaching wasn't yet in view. "Who is it? Who's out there?"

Aaron, the man that was seconds away from becoming my husband, before the beast had attacked, stepped into the door-frame. He bowed slightly, and I watched his Adam's apple bob as he swallowed hard. "My lady, I just wanted to check on you and see if you are feeling better."

I frowned. In all the confusion about the miraculous recovery, I hadn't stopped to think about the fact that when I was attacked, the man who was supposed to be my protector for the rest of my life had fled. "You left me there."

"I thought you were right behind me," he said. "I had no weapons, you can't expect me to fight a creature like that with my bare hands."

"Is this how you'll defend me when I'm your wife?" I asked.

"They haven't told you," he said, his voice small.

"Told me what?" I asked.

"The priests, and your father, have agreed that due to the circumstances the marriage is complete without the sharing of the vows."

"That can't be," I said. The rules and ceremonies around weddings were very clear. The entire ceremony had to be performed, didn't it?

"They say, as soon as we consummate, it will be official in the eyes of the gods."

I tensed, pulling my knees up to my chest to close myself off from him. He couldn't possibly be here to claim me in that way right now. After everything I'd been through. The thought of it made me want to gag.

Aaron took a step back, raising his hands in mock surrender. "Of course I'm not here for that. Not now, we can do that when you're ready. We have time. Your father has granted me permission to take you home now that you are healed." He looked like a sad little boy. Lost, confused. I wondered if his family was pulling the strings as much as my own. It only made my dislike of him and my dislike of this marriage deepen.

I shook my head. "I'm not well enough to travel yet."

He bowed again. "Of course, my dear. It's probably best for you to rest another day or two and then we can leave. I will make sure that you recover in the lap of luxury. I will keep soldiers posted at your door at all times to make sure you stay safe from harm."

Soldiers placed at my door at all times didn't sound like something that was being done for my own benefit. That sounded like something you did to someone who was your prisoner or someone you didn't trust. "Am I to be trapped in my own home?"

Aaron's eyes widened, clearly surprised by my boldness.

I didn't back down. Dropping my feet back to the ground, I stood and lifted my chin. "I'm not sure what you were promised, but I will not be a prisoner."

Aaron's hands were shaking and disgust tumbled through me. This was the man who was supposed to be my protector? He was nothing but a coward and I had a feeling that if I left here with him, I would be another pawn in another person's game.

I always knew my father was using me to advance his own ambitions, but I thought that once I had a husband, there may be some small speck of freedom I could gain. Now, looking at the sniveling boy in front of me, I knew that would never come to be. There was no way this weak fool was running his own lands. Someone else was pulling the strings. And what would happen when that person was gone? Would someone else step in? And how would they treat the wife of a man who fled when a beast attacked his bride on their wedding day?

I sat quietly hoping Aaron would leave my room. I didn't want to deal with him and I knew I didn't want to end up a day's ride away from the woods where Nani said I could find a way into Faerie.

It still didn't seem real, and it still seemed like it might not be the best decision. I stared silently at Aaron while I thought about Nani's words. The more I thought about it, the more appealing a life away from all of this sounded. Maybe I should chance it. Just run away to the woods and see what happened. The worst that could happen was death and to be honest, that might not be as bad as being locked up in the Baron's manor.

Finally, Aaron seemed to realize I wasn't going to say any more and without another word, he left my doorway.

Carefully, I pushed myself to standing and was pleasantly surprised to find that walking was a little bit easier than it had been. Hopefully that meant my strength was returning.

Making sure my dressing gown was tied around me, I tentatively stepped toward the door and left my room, hoping I could find some word on what my father was planning for Nani. I had to see if I could help her get out of there before he completed whatever spectacle it was that he intended for her. I knew it wouldn't be something he would come up with right away, I knew he would want to make an example of her. Anything he could do to draw attention and affection from the crowd, anything to stoke his own ego.

I tiptoed through the halls, sticking to the areas where rugs covered the creaking wood floors as much as I could. Hushed voices floated toward me and I followed them to my father's study. Keeping as quiet as possible, I crept nearer to his private chambers.

The door had been left open, not something I typically saw my father do. Either he was rushed, or the person joining had left the door open on purpose. The crack wasn't large enough for me to see through, but it might be enough for me to hear what he was saying.

I pressed my ear against the door while trying not to topple into it. My father was in the room with at least one other man and I couldn't make out every word, but there were occasional pieces of the conversation I could hear. Words like: money, land, and merchants. None of the words were uncommon in our house, my father was constantly trying to increase the revenue from his business. Then, I heard my name.

I held my breath, and pushed open the door just a little. The hinges were well oiled and didn't make a sound. I blew out the breath slowly, relieved. I could see inside the room better now and was able to make out my father's face and the back of another man's head. I wasn't sure who the man was, as it wasn't someone I had seen before. Then, I realized there was a third figure and my blood ran cold. Aaron was part of this conversation. Whatever they were discussing had to do with my marriage.

"I don't know if it's worth the money," the unknown man said.

"It's more money than either of us could ever dream of, you know that," my father said.

"Uncle, I told you I can handle her," Aaron leaned forward and I could see his face now, previously hidden in the position of the door. My heart thumped against my rib cage and the hair on the back of my neck stood on edge.

"You're not going to win over a wife by fleeing like a scared child," the man who I now knew was Aaron's uncle said.

I smirked, agreeing with him.

"What was I supposed to do? Would you rather I died trying to protect that creature?" he said.

My brow furrowed. I thought he had been referring to me, but why would he call me a creature?

"I told you," my father said. "This is a long game. My contact with the faeries said she's of value. They said we have to keep her alive. Getting her into your iron house will trap her. You only have to keep her locked up until her birthday. Then, she'll be fully human and you get the dowry you were promised," my father said.

I felt like the wind had been knocked from my lungs and my vision blurred for a moment. Had he just said what I thought he said? Was my father confirming Nani's story? Had he always known? Who was paying them to keep me locked up? It was like all my worst fears coming to fruition. Nothing felt real anymore.

"This isn't what I signed up for," Aaron said. "It's bad enough that I'm expected to start a family with a Fae. Now, you're telling me I have to risk my life to keep it alive?"

The amount of contempt in his voice made my skin crawl. He didn't see me as a person. He didn't even see me as a possession as my father did, he saw me as something disgusting. No wonder he did not even try to help me. He was afraid of me.

"She'll only be Fae a few months longer," my father said.

I took a step back away from the door as a million thoughts raced through my mind colliding with each other, making me more confused by the second. Who else knew? Why had this been kept from me? Was Nani in on this the whole time? She'd encouraged the wedding at first. What made her change her mind? Maybe they wanted me to run, maybe that was part of the plan.

I took another backward step and the floor creaked under my foot. I froze and felt the blood drain from my face.

Internally, I knew I needed to run, but I couldn't make myself do it. The door in front of me flew open and three angry faces glared at me.

"How much did you hear?" my father asked.

"Enough," I said. "I don't want to be a pawn in your game. I'm done. I'm leaving." I spun on my heels, intending to march to my room to put on proper traveling clothes. Before I got more than a few steps away a hand closed in around my upper arm locking me in place.

"You're not going anywhere," my father said. "You're married. You belong to him. As soon as the horses are ready, you're traveling to the Baron's manor, where you'll stay."

I pulled away from his grip, yanking my arm away from him. "I'm not going anywhere."

Chapter Six

Someone grabbed me by my dressing gown, but I kept running forward. They pulled harder, dragging me backward. Quickly, I untied the belt on the gown and lunged forward, pulling my arms from the sleeves as I raced away.

Another set of arms was around my waist before I could get to the stairway. I was thrown to the ground, my nose slammed into the wood floor sending stinging pain through my cheeks and into my eyes. I whimpered and tried to roll over to my back so I could see my attacker. I managed to turn enough to see that Aaron was the one who was holding me down.

"You're pathetic, you know that?" I spat at him.

He wiped his face off and glared down at me. "You think I want to waste my time with you?"

I lifted my leg swiftly, kicking Aaron in the groin. He fell onto his knees, face scrunched up in agony. He let go of me and sat down on the ground, grabbing his injured manhood.

I scrambled to my feet and ran again, only to be stopped this time by my own father blocking my path. "Let me go, I'll leave this place. I'll never come back."

"Oh no, this marriage means a great deal to this family. The people who raised you. It's the least you can do for the food we fed you and the clothes we put on your back." He glared at me, as if he were looking at a stranger.

I swallowed against the lump in my throat. There was little I could do to deny Nani's words, this man wasn't my father, but I had believed he was my whole life. How did you just go back on nineteen years of thinking one thing and suddenly think something else?

The same could be said for him, though. How long had it been an act? Was this why Rose had always been so adored while I was simply endured? A streak of defiance shot through me and I found the strength to clench my fists and stare him down. "Just let me go."

He shook his head. "I'm sorry, but they're paying me too much to keep you alive."

"Who?" I asked.

Suddenly, searing pain spread through me as someone tightened something around my waist. I looked down, to see chains wrapping around my lower arms, pinning them in place against my body. Where the chains touched bare flesh, I felt like I was on fire. I screamed in agony as whoever was holding them tightened them around me.

"Ease up, we need her alive," someone said.

My vision blurred and the pain made it so difficult to concentrate, I couldn't pinpoint who was speaking.

Swaying, I fought the urge to vomit as consciousness slipped away. Shaking my head, I tried to maintain some sense of myself, to fight against the increasing pain. The last thing I needed to do was pass out again.

I wasn't sure what they would do to me or where they would take me if I slipped away. I knew I needed to fight, I had to get away from here now. They had plans to keep me locked up and if they moved me too far from the woods how would I ever find where I needed to be? The hatred and disgust in their conversation just proved how much I had to get to the woods.

Something clawed at the back of my mind, aching to break free. Every time this had happened in the past, I'd suppressed it, afraid that something was wrong with me. This time, I embraced it, calling to whatever it was.

Get me out of here, I thought. I needed an escape. Something to break free of this. I screamed, fighting against the pain, using the last bit of my strength to push away from my captors.

A sudden burst of light filled the room, temporarily blinding me. I gasped as the chains fell from me, the searing agony of them slipping away as they landed with a rattle on the ground. I jumped over them, needing to put as much space between me and those evil bindings as possible.

Still nauseous and shaky, I knew this was my chance. I stumbled as I lurched forward, still feeling the burning memory of the chains on my skin. Hands stretched out in front of me, I moved as fast as I could through the achingly blinding light. My fingers traced the walls and the paintings and the tapestries that I had walked by a million times in this place I called home. Now, the only thing I wanted to do was get away.

Screams of confusion and pain and anger sounded behind me and my heart hammered wildly. Every step was agony as anxiety clenched my insides. I had to find the door first, I had to get free of this house. I had a feeling, that if I let them get me now, it was over for me.

A few more steps and my palms hit a dead end. I felt around frantically, trying to figure out where the doorway was. I turned around in the hallway and squinted, trying to see more clearly.

My eyes were adjusting or the light was fading. Either way, I could now see the door. I ran forward, toward the woods, ignoring the cries behind me from my father and the man claiming to be my husband.

I wasn't sure what I was going to do when I reached the

woods. All I knew was that nothing in my life was what I thought it was. The only thing that made sense was to follow Nani's directions. I wasn't sure if I fully trusted her, but I knew I would take her word over anyone who wanted to lock me up. She was the only one who had been there for me as a child and Nani's last words to me were to go to the woods.

Grief flooded through me as I made my escape, praying I wasn't condemning Nani in the process. I knew if I went back for her, I wouldn't escape again. I also knew that she would tell me to run. She wouldn't want me to risk myself to save her but my heart ached leaving her there. I hoped she had magic, something she could use to escape.

My bare feet flew across the grass of the gardens that surrounded our home. Bright summer sun shone down on me as if mocking the horror I was going through right then. If the weather were to imitate the way my insides felt, it would be a tumbling, windy thunderstorm. Beads of sweat slid down my back and my lungs burned, but I pressed on, focused on the forest ahead.

The trees in the distance looked like sanctuary. I knew my father and Aaron were probably chasing me, but I didn't look back. I pumped my arms harder, my chest stinging with exertion, my legs burning. I just needed to get a few more steps, I was so close I could taste the pine, I could almost feel the cool water of the stream, and I could smell my freedom.

I saw the figures standing in the forest too late to slow down or turn to avoid them. Instead, I crashed right into two strangers who instantly grabbed hold of me. I'd managed to escape one group of men, only to be captured by another. I wasn't going to let them stop me.

Kicking and screaming, I clawed at the face of the man who was holding me up against his chest. I scratched, and hissed like a lynx defending its territory. He tightened his grip, squeezing me in closer to his body, pinning my arms against my side.

I kicked at his shins, but he didn't budge at my attempts to escape. "Let me go!"

"Easy, we're not going to hurt you," he said, leaning down so his mouth was against my ear.

Involuntarily, I whimpered, feeling defeated in his unbreakable grasp. "Please. Just let me go."

"Shhh, everything is going to be fine," he said. His voice was soothing, calming, like a spring breeze.

I took a deep breath, catching the scent of rosemary and honey. My body relaxed momentarily and he eased his grip on me. I tried to press against him, a last attempt at freedom, but even with the lessened grip, I didn't budge. Feeling defeated, my shoulders dropped.

"We are trying to help you," another male voice said.

"Is that what you call it?" I asked. "Do you hold everyone you try to help against their will?"

"I like the fire in her," the man who was holding me said.

I looked up at him and focused on his face for the first time. He had a strong chiseled jaw and smiled at me with full lips. His bright green eyes seemed to sparkle in the sunlight and stray dark brown hair fell in a messy pile onto his forehead. I opened my mouth to speak, but my gaze remained fixated on my captor. It wasn't possible for someone to be that attractive. I squirmed against his chest and realized I could feel the muscles below his tunic. Whoever this man was, he was strong.

"I will put you down now, but you need to promise not to run," he said.

That's when I realized, my feet weren't touching the ground. My captor lowered me and took his hands away from me.

I looked up, surprised to find that the handsome man was a whole head, maybe even two taller than me. I'd always been tall for a woman, but this man made me feel petite, not an easy feat. I looked to my right to be greeted by another equally attractive man.

The man on my right had bronze, sun kissed skin and warm brown eyes. His long dark hair was plaited into a braid behind his head giving me a clear view of his pointed ears.

I gasped. "You're not human." I felt foolish saying those words out loud because it was painfully clear now that I looked at them again. No human male was this tall, or this strong, or this beautiful. "Your ears. You're Fae."

"That we are," the male who had been holding me said.

I blinked a few times, looking at each of them in turn. My breathing slowed as I stood there letting it sink in.

"That's better, see now we can talk about things like civilized people," the first male said. "I'm Dane, and this is Cormac."

"I don't understand what's happening," I said.

"We're not exactly sure ourselves, love," Dane said.

Now that I'd calmed down, I could tell they didn't intend to harm me. Both males were wearing weapons on their belts, yet their hands were free from weapons. If they wanted to hurt me, they could have done so easily. Instead, they were standing there with ease, talking to me. It seemed too much of a coincidence for them to be here in light of Nani's revelation. But I wasn't sure if their arrival was connected to my departure. "What are you doing here and why did you stop me?"

"We were chasing a monster," Cormac said. "It led us here."

"Imagine our surprise when we saw a Fae about to wed a mortal," Dane said.

"Are you talking about me?" I asked even though I already knew the answer. Hearing it from Nani and hearing it from my father should have been enough for it to sink in by now. But it was so hard to believe. Even with two Fae males standing in front of me it was still shocking. How could I be one of them? They all had an otherworldly glow to them, matching pointed ears, and a beauty I'd never seen on a human.

"Yes, we're talking about you," Cormac said.

As far as I knew, I didn't look anything like them but I had a sinking feeling in the pit of my stomach that told me something had changed. Holding my breath, I reached up and felt my ears. Sure enough, there was a point to them that hadn't been there before. I swallowed hard.

"I highly recommend you let us take you back to Faerie. I'm not sure what you're doing here, but I can tell you it's not going to turn out well for you if you stay. Those boorish humans are headed this way, probably bearing pitchforks."

"You want me to go with you?" I asked.

"Well, I assume you want to figure out why you're here as much as we do. If you were taken from Faerie, we have to get the Queen involved. This could mean war against the humans," he said.

"No, there's no reason to jump to war. I've always lived here. My maid, she told me I was a changeling, that she hid me here," I said.

"That's not possible," Dane said. "They outlawed changelings."

"It doesn't matter," Cormac said. "We're taking her back with us. She doesn't belong here and she's in danger. We'll figure out the rest when we get there."

"Ready?" Cormac asked Dane.

"Autumn Court?" Dane asked.

Cormac nodded.

"Wait, what's happening?" I asked.

"We're going to slide. It's the fastest way to travel," Cormac said.

Before I had a chance to consent, he wrapped his arm around my waist and a gust of wind rushed past me, circling me and stealing my breath. A moment later, I felt weightless and my vision was dotted with starlight.

Just as quickly as it had come, the darkness vanished, and my feet were back on solid ground. My face heated as I realized I was hanging onto the Fae for dear life. Sure that fear was etched into every furrow of my brow, I looked up at him, hoping for some reassurance.

"We're here, you can let go of me now," he said.

I dropped my arms from him and stepped away, feeling like a frightened child who was just told that monsters didn't exist. The difference was, I now knew monsters did exist.

Chapter Seven

Trees with fiery red and glowing orange leaves stood in stark contrast against the steely gray sky. A biting chill hung in the air, though it wasn't exactly cold. A gentle breeze rustled the leaves, creating a symphony of whistling and rustling. I took a deep breath in, the air smelled of cinnamon and wood smoke, reminding me of a perfect fall day at home.

I knew this wasn't home, there was something about this place, something that made it too wonderful for it to be the human realm. Without asking, I knew we were in Faerie. "How did you do that?"

"You have much to learn," Cormac said.

"You were there when the monster attacked, weren't you?" I asked.

The males nodded.

The arrows flying through the air had saved me. I now knew they didn't belong to any of the men my father had invited to the wedding, they had belonged to one of these Fae. They had saved my life when my own family had fled. "Thank you."

"We wouldn't let an innocent die by beast," Cormac said with a shrug.

"But you didn't have to come back for me, either," I said. "Why did you?"

"Curiosity, honor, something like that," Dane said with a shrug.

I tried not to let him see the disappointment at the answer he'd given. It wasn't that I expected strangers to come in and save me from my fate, but after finding out that I was one of them, I'd hoped for some bond that made them want to help me.

A red and gold butterfly flew across my vision and I let go of the disappointment. I was here now and I was safe from whatever plans my father and the Baron had for me. Whatever the Fae interest was in me, it had to be better. At least I had to hope it was. I followed the butterfly with my eyes and once again found myself drawn into the scenery around me. "It's so beautiful."

"Welcome to Faerie," Dane said.

"We need to get her out of here," Cormac said. "I think we need to take her to see Angela."

"I'll still never understand what you saw in her," Dane said.

"And I still say it's none of your business," Cormac said. "She's neutral, and you know it's the safest place for us to go. If I brought a changeling to my house..." he didn't finish the sentence.

"Can you just explain to me what's going on here? Why is it so terrible that I exist?" I asked.

"Changelings were outlawed about a century ago by the Queen herself," Dane said. "Too many Fae families were using them in rather unethical ways."

I wasn't sure I wanted to hear all of the details about that. So I shut my mouth, and followed the Fae males down the road. We walked about five minutes before I realized how strange we must appear to anyone who might see us. Though, to be fair, we hadn't passed a single structure or another living creature since we arrived.

The winding path was made of pressed dirt and looked like it was well cared for. It didn't look like it had been worn by travelers, but rather placed there on purpose. The trees that lined the path didn't have a single dead branch, nothing out of place. The wind whispered through them creating a gentle shaking sound that trailed us as we walked. I scanned the trees, looking for any signs of life. No rabbit, no chipmunks, no critters at all. I shivered, hugging myself to keep warm. I was still dressed in my thin nightclothes.

"What is this place?" I asked.

"Where we are is not important," Cormac said.

"Why are we alone? Why are there no other animals or faeries or homes?" I asked.

"This is my family's land," Cormac said. He turned away from me and continued to walk, clearly not willing to elaborate.

For someone who seemed so disinterested in bringing me to his home, I was surprised that he had taken us straight to his property. Glancing around again, I looked for any signs of buildings. All I could see were trees.

"How much land does your family have?"

"Technically," Dane said, "all of it."

"All of what? All of Faerie?" I asked.

Dane laughed. "No, not all of Faerie, though I'm sure his father wishes."

I continued to walk, not acknowledging Dane's comment. I was still feeling completely confused and lost but I didn't know what else I was supposed to do. Going back home wasn't an option. I had no money, no food, no friends in the world as far as I knew. These strangers were probably the best shot I had at survival. Though I wasn't quite sure what survival was going to look like if I stayed with them.

I wondered if I should ask them to take me back. Maybe I could try and join the Temple, then I realized if they found out what I was, I would be just as unsafe there as I was anywhere else in the mortal world. No, my days of living with humans were over. Even if I did feel like I belonged there more than here. I hoped that would change since I never fully felt at home there. It would be nice to belong somewhere.

The longer we walked, the more exhaustion set in. I'd been through a lot in the last two days and I was unused to walking long distances. It wasn't something women did. We weren't allowed to hunt or wander off alone. The time I got to spend riding was a rare luxury that allowed me to build up quite a bit of stamina, but the muscles used for that clearly didn't transfer over.

Either that, or I was still recovering from the seemingly healed injury. I wanted to ask them about that; I wanted to ask hundreds of questions. I had a feeling I wasn't going to get any answers until we got to our destination. So, I stared at the trees as we walked, trying to fill my senses with the beauty of the place.

I was grateful for the soft dirt beneath my bare feet and the warm sunshine that cut through the chill in the air. I probably should've been feeling self-conscious of the fact that I was wearing so little, but neither of the males seemed to notice. I'd only been here less than an hour, I hadn't seen any other people or faeries, but I could already tell this place was very different than the human world I'd grown up in.

Ahead, I thought I saw a shadow behind some of the slender tree trunks and adrenaline spiked in my gut. I stopped walking and stared at the movements of the tree. The shadow passed by again, independently of the sun. Something was definitely there.

"What is it?" Dane asked.

"I think there's something in the trees," I said.

Dane pulled his bow from his back and nocked an arrow. Cormac followed suit, and both of them turned toward the shadow, moving slowly. Watching them with weapons drawn made me think back to my monster encounter. Arrows from these men had saved me that day.

I was grateful they'd been out hunting yesterday, otherwise I'd be dead right now. The memory of the claws digging into my side flashed through my mind. I took a step back, wanting to distance myself farther from what I was sure was going to be a repeat of yesterday's encounter.

I heard a snarl behind me and I felt warm air blowing through the thin fabric of my night shirt. My skin tingled in fear as I slowly turned around.

Breathing down on me, was another beast. Before I could scream, the creature grabbed me, pulling me up against its hairy body. Every inch of me tensed and I froze in fear, unable to speak. Breathing down on me, with the scent of death on its breath, I gagged. Regaining control, I screamed, then kicked my feet against its furry midsection, trying to free myself from the creature.

I could feel its claws resting against my skin, the slightest amount of pressure from his grip would send them into me. As I struggled, one of the claws broke my skin. I gasped as pain shot through me and I stopped struggling, knowing that if I continued to move more of the deadly talons would end up in my flesh.

In front of me, the Fae males were surrounded by three additional creatures. Two of them already had several arrows sticking out of their hides. The third, was swiping at Cormac who had abandoned his bow for a sword.

I had never wished for a weapon any more than I did at this moment. If I was going to stay in Faerie, in these dangerous lands, I was going to need to learn how to defend myself. That was, if I could get away from the beast.

With my free hand, I reached up and scratched the beast's face, hoping I could catch it off guard. It shrank back and shook its head, looking more annoyed than harmed. Then it tightened its grip on me again, sending more claws piercing my flesh.

Stars danced in front of my vision as I fought to stay awake against the pain. The creature spread its wings, and I struggled against its grip again. Once more, each movement pushed claws farther into me.

Taking shallow breaths, I tried to think of a way out of this.

Nothing came to mind. Feeling lightheaded, I looked for the Fae who had saved me once before, hoping one of them was coming to rescue me again. I hated feeling so helpless, but I was running out of energy. Even breathing was painful now.

Two of the creatures lay on the ground, unmoving while Cormac swung his sword at the third. Dane was running toward me. Maybe he could get this thing to let me go. The creature holding me repositioned me, pulling me closer to its snout. Saliva dripped all over my face. I wiped it away but even that action caused the creature's grip to tighten around me.

Desperate, I cried out to Dane, "Help, please!"

The creature lifted me higher, so my face was now at the same level as its own, creating new puncture wounds as claws gripped previously uninjured flesh.

Dane stopped running and nocked an arrow into his bow. A flutter of hope rose in my chest as he released the arrow. It hit the monster somewhere behind me, causing it to roar in anger. I wiggled, trying to free myself in the midst of the attack. The claws dug into me with every movement and I bit down on my lip to keep from screaming.

Instead of letting go of me, the monster tightened its grip and in a rush of wind, it leapt from the ground, spreading its wings wide, catching the air and flapping away from my would-be rescuers.

Tears slid down my cheeks and I hoped whatever this creature was doing with me, it would set me down so I would have a chance to run. That was, if I didn't bleed to death or get dropped first. Below, the ground was a patchwork of red and gold, dotted by crystal blue lakes and a few yellow meadows. Wind whipped through my hair, undoing any of the remaining work that Nani had done to prepare me for my wedding day. How had that only been yesterday?

Just yesterday, my greatest concern was marrying a stranger and losing my freedom. Today, I learned I wasn't even human, and as blood seeped into my white night clothes, I knew I was fighting for my life. Again. When Nani had told me stories about the Fae, I had romanticized them. Now, I was more inclined to agree with Rose and her fear of the creatures and the unknown found in the Faerie realm.

Chapter Eight

✦✦✦

The creature shifted again sending a shockwave of agony that radiated across my body. I took a quick intake of breath and blew it out forcing myself to stay focused on the landscape below me.

To my right I spotted a river that cut through the trees and grassy meadows, all the way back near the location we had come from. I looked for any other landmarks that could help me get to that river if I were able to escape. If I could follow it, maybe I could get back to where I had left my rescuers.

I shook my head, feeling foolish. What were the chances they'd be waiting there? That wouldn't make any sense. They were either tracking this creature, and coming to save me, or presumed I was dead already and were moving on about their business.

A shudder ran down my spine at the thought of being abandoned once again. My own husband-to-be had run off when one of these monsters attacked, why would I think these strangers were any different?

Then, I recalled they had said they were hunting these beasts. It was possible they'd track this creature if that were still the case. I wondered if there was anything I could do to this creature to cause it to go down without killing me in the process. Before I could think of anything, the monster's wings slowed their flapping and we sank lower in the sky.

The trees and plants below us came into sharper focus, merging together as we neared the ground. We were near a rocky hillside that didn't have the same color or vibrancy as the place I had been snatched from. Hastily, I was dropped on top of the hill, landing hard. A cloud of dirt rose around me and I coughed, fanning the dirt away so I could see better.

The pain of being dropped was nothing compared to the relief I felt at not having those terrible claws shoved in my side. No sooner than it had dropped me, the beast flew away, leaving me alone on a pile of rocks.

Forcing myself to stand, I leaned against a boulder to keep myself from falling over. That's when I noticed that I was on a small ledge rather high up. I had no idea why I'd been taken there, but I didn't want to wait around to find out.

As best I could, I assessed the damage from the claws. Once again I was covered in my own blood. This wasn't something I hoped I was going to have to get used to here. The injury burned, but the blood seemed to be slowing on its own already. I knew if I didn't get proper treatment, I wasn't going to make it. Either that, or I'd be eaten as soon as the monster returned.

I took a few careful steps hanging onto anything that seemed secure enough to support me as I did so as not to fall over. The hilltop or small mountain or whatever I was on, was about twice the height of my childhood home, which had been two stories. It wasn't the highest hill I'd seen, but as I glanced down I realized there wasn't an easy route to the ground.

The steep hill was covered in jagged rocks, making it a tricky descent by foot or a blind and risky plunge to the ground. If I jumped, I would end up broken and battered from the rocks I'd smash into on the way down. There no way I would survive. The only way down, was either flying, which wasn't happening, or taking tiny careful steps hoping that I didn't slip.

Despite the dizziness and the blood loss, I wasn't willing to wait for the creature to return. Climbing down was my only shot at survival. Even if the Fae males were coming to rescue me, who knew if they'd arrive before the monster did.

I tore the fabric from the bottom of my shirt and the legs of my pants, doing my best to maintain some dignity, to make bandages to attempt to staunch the bleeding. Then, on aching and bloodied feet, I began the treacherous descent.

I was a few steps down, when I lost my footing and slid, leaving me dangling by my hands over the drop off. Swinging myself up as best I could, I used my knees to gain hold of some of the rocks before I could place my feet on something steady.

I looked back up, hoping I'd made it further than I thought. Unfortunately, I only descended about one body length. Sweat trickled down my brow and stung my eyes as I carefully repositioned my footing. Breathing heavy, and now seeing double, I tried to trick myself into pretending the pain didn't exist. *When this was over, if I survived this, I had to find a bath and stay there for a week.* I would need the rest, and I needed to wash away all of this dirt.

Day dreaming about sitting in warm lavender scented water, I ignored the sharp pains in my feet as I found purchase in my descent. Slowly, I continued to move. Focusing on making sure my grip was steady before I continued.

I reached my toes down stretching below me to find the next place I could rest them, and was surprised by the touchdown on a ledge wide enough for me to stand. After getting both feet on there, I loosened my grip and leaned against the side of the rock taking a much needed rest.

My heart was pounding; my breathing came in short bursts. I closed my eyes and focused on steadying myself as I prepared for another round of climbing. I allowed myself a minute to catch my breath, and though I still wasn't returned to normal, I didn't want to wait any longer.

Slowly and carefully I began again, rocks biting into my bare feet, hands slipping on loose stones, fear spiking every time the ground shifted underneath of me.

I was determined to make it down, but dark thoughts started to get in my way. After I made it down, then what? I was alone, I was injured, and I was in a strange place. Desperation and defeat crowded around me like a thick fog I had to cut through with each step. Somehow, I was going to make it through this and then I would figure out what to do next. I had to. I hadn't come this far to give up now.

I was going through the motions more easily now, finding a rhythm, but my body was resisting. My fingers tingled and my toes were numb. I wasn't sure how much longer I could take when finally, I touched down at the bottom.

I knew I should run, I knew I should get as far away from there as I could, but I had nothing left.

I collapsed, my arms hanging limp at my sides. Every inch of my skin was covered with either blood or sweat; my hair stuck to my forehead and the back of my neck.

I'd felt tired when I woke up after the first attack, but this was a whole different level of exhaustion.

The sound of wings flapping through the air followed by a loud screeching cry shook me from my momentary fog. I looked around, knowing I didn't have enough energy to go far, but hoping I could find a place to hide.

There was a grove of trees not too far off and also tall plants that reminded me of the cattails we had back home. My heart leaped at the thought of water so close by.

Dragging myself to my feet, I stumbled forward, hoping I could make it to the trees and then continue toward the tall plants that might get me to fresh water. The only thing keeping me going was the promise of cool, soothing water on my aching limbs. Even fear wasn't enough to get my body moving across the ground, I was too tired to feel afraid anymore.

A roar sounded above me again, and I didn't even look up. At this point, if the creature dove to try to get me, I didn't stand a chance. There was no fight left in me.

I stumbled into the trees, leaning against the first one I reached. From there, I could smell the sweetness of the familiar scent of moss and wet rocks. Sliding to the bottom of the tree, I had to push myself to standing again before staggering forward.

Now that I was moving, I realized the marshy area was farther than I originally thought. Cursing my decision, I considered turning back and hiding among the trees.

Then I heard the sound of soft rushing water and it was enough to make me continue forward. When I reached the tall grasses, I parted them and climbed inside the grove of cattails. The temperature dropped instantly as my sore feet sank into soft, soothing mud. I let out a long sigh of relief as some of the pressure and pain eased with each step.

As I approached the water, tears slid down my cheeks. This water represented hope, a chance of cleansing my wounds and a chance at survival. The river in front of me wasn't even a real river, it was barely a stream. But it had clear rushing water and I stepped right in the current without even pausing to consider how deep it might be. A few steps in, and the water rose to my knees.

I sank down, leaning my head back, and began washing off all of the dirt and blood. I pulled off my night clothes, which were nothing more than scraps at that point anyway, and laid them out on some stones to dry in the sun.

As I scrubbed the blood from the wounds, I noticed they were already healing. As confused as I was, I was grateful for the gift that seem to accompany my newfound heritage. Now wasn't the time to question the magic that was going to help me stay alive for another day.

I leaned back in the pool of water, letting the ripples rush past me and I thought back to my childhood. Had I always healed so quickly? I tried to think of a time I'd been sick or hurt, and I couldn't pinpoint a single instance. I remembered one winter, when Rose almost died from fever, and my parents separated us so I wouldn't catch the illness. Despite the fact that several children in our community died that year, including one of my best playmates, and Rose fought for her life in the weeks the illness took over her body, I never even had so much as a sniffle.

Nani had said that changeling children were stripped of their magic, but maybe some of it had survived in the human world, after all. I took a deep breath, closed my eyes and said a silent prayer to whichever goddess would hear me for Nani. *Please keep her safe.*

Then, I opened my eyes and looked around. There was nobody there to keep me safe. I was going to have to figure out what to do next on my own.

Chapter Nine

✻

I sank back into the cold, rushing water and ran my fingers through my hair, working out some of the knots. I was going to have to leave the water and find shelter before the sun set. Looking over at the tattered remains of my wet night clothes, I frowned. They weren't going to be much use to me even if they were dry.

I glanced around, hoping for some sign of civilization. Why did this land seem so desolate? Beautiful, yes, but apparently so sparsely populated that I hadn't seen any sign of a home or other being since my arrival. When I was flying, I recalled seeing what looked like fields and farmland, but I couldn't recall seeing the typical homes I'd seen growing up. Perhaps I'd been too high up to notice. Or too terrified.

With a sigh, I picked up my sopping clothing and pulled on the remains of my white pants. They only covered my upper thighs after I'd torn them and they were see through now, thanks to the water, but they'd dry on me just the same as they would on a rock. I was too cold to sit in the water and there was no way I was going to walk around naked. I gasped as I tugged my shirt over my head as the cold soggy fabric clung to my skin. My waist was exposed, but at least my breasts were covered. Not that anything was truly hidden under the sheer fabric.

Wrapping my arms over my chest, I waded through the water back to shore. Standing on the bank, I took a moment to try to orient myself. My best bet was to take the same path back that the bat beast had flown. I knew if I followed that route, I'd be exposed and in clear line of sight if the creature was still hunting me. Frustrated, I pushed the stuck strands of my long hair away from my forehead and dropped my arms to my side. How much easier would it be to just curl up into a little ball here and go to sleep? I wasn't sure how I was going to cross back to where I'd come from and there didn't seem to be anything around.

I looked at the stream behind me and knelt down, peeking at the flow of the water. It seemed to pick up speed as it raced away from me at a steady decline. It was possible the little stream would become a wider river. My education had been minimal, but I knew that where there was water, there would be crops.

I stood and brushed the dirt from my hands. There was no point in trying to get back to where I had come from. What I needed was a warm room and a hearty meal. That wasn't something I'd get from the middle of nowhere. Instead, I'd follow the stream. That way, if I got lost, at least I could find my way back to where I started. It wasn't a great plan, but it was the best I had.

As I walked, I peeked at the scrapes and injuries on my body. The scratches on my arms and legs were healed and the puncture marks from the claws were nearly healed. Being Fae was certainly not all bad. I might be ostracized from my family, though they brought that on themselves as far as I was concerned, and I might not have any idea what I was going to do, but I was alive. So I would walk until I found someone to take me in for the night.

After what felt like miles of silence, hoof beats thundered into range. My shoulders lifted and I turned toward the direction of the sound. I'd stayed in the undergrowth surrounding the stream and couldn't see the road, but I knew it had to be there.

Risking being seen, I peeked out through the cattails to see what was heading this way. It was a single rider, but I couldn't determine what he or she looked like.

I squinted into the sunlight, trying to make out the details of the rider silhouetted against the setting sun. Had it been a whole day already? Maybe time worked differently there.

I held my breath for a second, trying to decide if it was better to stay hidden, or approach the rider for help. I stared down at my tattered shreds of clothing and tried to figure out how many hours of sunlight I even had left. At the rate I was going, I would freeze to death the second the sun sank below the horizon.

Wrapping my arms tighter around my chest to give myself the illusion of privacy, I climbed out from between the cattails and walked onto the main road.

I hoped the rider was a kind person or Fae or whatever. At that moment, my fate seemed to rest in the hands of the rider and the horse trotting down the road toward me.

I could make out male features now, dark hair and luminous skin. Definitely Fae. He had a strong build under a well fitted tunic. The black horse he rode was a powerful animal that would have been the envy of anyone in the town I grew up in. With every smooth stride, the creature's muscles flexed and rippled in the sunlight showing the shine of the well cared for coat.

The rider slowed as he approached me, and all too soon, I found myself face-to-face with a stranger.

"Are you lost?" The rider smirked. He looked like he was holding back a laugh.

"What makes you think I'm lost? Perhaps I'm just going for a walk," I snapped. I knew I should just ask for help. I was at the point where I should probably beg for help, but the way his eyes sparkled and his lips turned upward made me feel like he was teasing me.

"Well, you're making quite a statement in those clothes. If I didn't know any better, I'd say maybe you needed some help," he said, hopping off his horse.

I swallowed hard and nodded once, dropping my guard. I had already resigned myself to asking for help, it shouldn't be this hard to follow through. "I just arrived, this is all I have."

The Fae turned toward his horse, pulled something out of a saddlebag before returning to me. A moment later, a cloak was wrapped over my shoulders and the dark-haired Fae leaned in close while he fastened it around my neck. This close, I could see how smooth his skin was and how strong his jaw was. He smelled like sandalwood and lemon and part of me wanted to bury myself into his chest. That wasn't a normal reaction for me when I met a man for the first time, and it startled me.

I took a step back the second he dropped his fingers from the cloak and looked up at him through my lashes. He was head and shoulders taller than me, once again making me feel small.

"I won't hurt you," he said. "My name's Ethan."

"Cassia," I said.

"Come on, I'll get you home," he said, offering his hand.

"I don't exactly have a home anymore," I said.

His brow furrowed. "You running from your master, husband, or father?"

I stopped walking and stared at him. "Is that something that happens often here?"

He shrugged. "Not really, but seeing as how you're alone with nothing, I have to wonder what you were in such a hurry to escape."

That made more sense. I sighed. "I ran from my wedding."

It seemed like enough to say. I hoped he would think I was afraid of the man I was to marry or wasn't in love with him. I occasionally heard stories of girls that would risk life on their own rather than marrying a terrible man. I never heard of those girls again, but I knew it happened from time to time. I wasn't sure what it said about me to him, but I had a feeling that keeping the fact that I was a changeling was probably the safest path for me.

Ethan looked like he wanted to comment, but he refrained. Instead, he offered his hand again and helped me onto his horse, then pulled himself up after me.

Strong arms wrapped around my waist, pulling my back up against his firm chest. Heat rose to my cheeks and I shuddered at his touch as tingles climbed down my back. I'd never been this close to a male before and I wondered if this was a normal reaction for me to have.

He leaned closer, his chin brushing against my forehead. "Don't worry, I've got you."

Grateful that he seemed to mistake my reaction to his proximity as nerves, I nodded.

He clicked his tongue and pulled up on the reins, and the horse took off at a gentle trot down the road.

I watched the river alongside the road, noting that it was widening as we traveled farther. There was something reassuring about knowing that I'd made the smartest choice when trying to save my life.

Since arriving in Faerie, I'd felt in even less control than I had in my father's house. Knowing that despite my lack of education, I had made a strong choice, gave me a spark of hope. *Perhaps I could make it work here.* Maybe it would all turn out for the best.

Some of the tension spilled from my shoulders in response to my newfound optimism. Turning away from the river, I looked ahead and was surprised to see a sprawling home in front of us. I'd been so close to reaching something when Ethan had come along. It made me wonder where he was headed and which task I'd stopped him from.

Polished black stones the size of my head now lined either side of the road, leading up to an impressive arched black stone entryway.

Ethan clicked his tongue again and his mount slowed as we crossed under the arch.

I looked around in awe. I'd never seen anything so grand and it was just a preview of what was to come. In front of me, was a brick and stone home with dark green shutters and a long stone entryway up to a pair of carved wood doors.

Vines climbed along one side of the house with bright green leaves that reached toward the fading sun and a neat row of flowers sat in pots under them.

I was so taken by the beauty of the place that I didn't realize Ethan had dismounted until he picked me up and lifted me from the horse as if I were a small child.

I yelped in surprise as he set me down, then bit down on my lower lip to curb the sound. "Thank you."

"You're welcome," he said. They were the first words he'd spoken since we started our ride and I had a feeling he was one of those rare men who preferred quiet.

"Where are we?" I whispered, suddenly overly aware of my own loud nature. "Do you live here?"

"No, I live in the Spring Court. This is my friend's home."

Before he could finish, the door opened and a familiar face walked through the door.

"Dane?" I asked.

"You've met?" Ethan asked, surprised.

Dane was tugging on a glove, but stopped when he saw me, causing the glove to fall to the ground. "We were just going back out to search again."

Neighing horses sounded behind me and I turned to see Cormac mounted on a steed, leading a second horse toward us.

"Cassia?" he asked, pulling back on the reins to stop his progress. He dismounted, then led the horses toward us.

"We found the creature's nest, but you weren't there," he said.

"I got away," I said, then winced at my lame response.

"How?" Dane asked.

A cool breeze ruffled the damp fabric that clung to my skin and I hugged myself as I tried to repress a shiver.

"That can wait," Ethan said. "Let's get her inside and cleaned up."

I was grateful for Ethan's concern and when he set his hand on the small of my back to usher me inside, I didn't hesitate. I was too tired, too cold, and too confused to resist the temptation of warmth and comfort.

Chapter Ten

I tiptoed across slick wood floors as I walked through the stunning entryway. Columns of wood carved with maple leaf designs separated us from a sitting room arranged around an especially large fireplace.

"Upstairs, second bedroom," Cormac called as Ethan continued to escort me through the home.

I caught sight of a slender female Fae in a blue dress and apron. She lowered her eyes away from me and inclined her head in a slight bow. It was a strange sensation to be given immediate status based on the fact that I was walking with Ethan. At least, I had to assume it came from that. My clothing wasn't exactly showing that I was someone who should be bowed to. Though my family's servants were supposed to do the same, they'd always been so relaxed around me. I only saw the formal behavior come out when my father was present.

Taking my eyes off of the servant, I followed Ethan up a flight of stairs. My feet sank into the plush rug that ran the entire length of the staircase. It was a deep burgundy carpet that felt softer than the silk of my ruined wedding dress. I wanted to curl up on one of the stairs and sink into the quiet softness of the cushion.

By the time we reached the bedroom, exhaustion had set in and I stared longingly at the canopy bed pushed up against the back wall.

"Wait here," Ethan said.

I nodded, and as soon as he walked through the door, I made my way over to the bed and sat down. My limbs felt like they were filled with sand. Giving in to the exhaustion, I fell back onto the bed with my legs dangling over the edge. Not having to hold up my own body weight was a relief and I let myself sink into the soft bedding. Closing my eyes, I took a deep breath in and realized that I felt safe there. I didn't know these people, but so far, they had only tried to help me. That was more than I could say about my own family.

My chest tightened at the thought. None of them were my family. I was alone. Emptiness swirled around my mind as I tried to grasp what any of this meant. I was a changeling. A Fae hidden from birth in a human household despite the fact that Faerie law didn't allow such a thing.

Pulling my legs up to my chest, I hugged them close to me and rolled onto my side. I had so many questions, but they were making me dizzy so I tried to clear my mind instead. I breathed in the scent of cedar and something sweet that I couldn't pinpoint.

Somewhere far away, I thought I heard my name, but I didn't answer. Instead, I took another deep breath then fell asleep.

I woke in a dark room, tangled in a pile of blankets I didn't remember covering myself with. My heart raced as I looked around the unfamiliar space. Then, I remembered I was in Faerie and I recalled sitting down on the bed while I was waiting for someone to return. *Ethan*. That was his name. My breathing slowed as I talked myself into releasing some of the tension I was holding in my balled fists. If the Fae males had any interest in harming me, they could have done so while I was sleeping. The fact that they hadn't didn't make me trust them, but it was enough to make me hope.

I threw the blankets from me and realized I was wearing different clothes. My torn nightgown was gone, replaced by what appeared to be an oversized green tunic. Flutters filled my chest as I realized it must belong to one of the males who lived here. I rolled the too long sleeves up, then looked around the room, wondering what I should do next.

Muted conversation carried through the closed door so I crept toward it. After my last encounter eavesdropping, my skin prickled in anticipation and fear as I carefully turned the door-knob. Holding my breath, I peeked around the open door hoping to hear some of what was being said before I announced that I was awake to the household.

The conversation ceased and I froze, worried I'd made a noise that had given me away.

"Cassia," Ethan's voice carried up to me. "You don't have to hide in there."

My face heated. How did he know I'd been standing there? I licked my lips and pushed the door open the rest of the way, determined not to let him know how uncomfortable I was.

I walked to the stairway to find all three Fae males waiting for me. I hesitated in my step for a second before continuing the descent. "How did you know I was awake?"

"After what you've been through we thought it best if I kept a closer eye on you," Ethan said.

The males moved aside as I reached the bottom of the stairway and I stopped in the middle of them. "What do you mean by that?"

He shrugged. "We all have different gifts, talents as it were. One of mine is the ability to forge connections with other Fae."

"Connections?" I asked, letting the word hang between us.

"I can sense where you are," he said.

"Is that necessary?" It seemed like a serious violation of privacy, though I could guess that most human men would wish for the skill to do the same. The idea of him being able to track me at all times made me want to head right for the front door.

"Don't even think about it," Cormac said, moving between me and the exit.

"And you do what, exactly? Read my mind?" I asked.

"No, I have no such gift," he said. "But you did get suddenly fixated on the door."

"So I'm a prisoner here?" I asked.

"Prisoner?" Dane laughed. "After we save her life, she calls herself a prisoner."

My cheeks flushed. They had saved my life, but I didn't understand why they'd bothered or why I was here. "Sorry."

"I'm sure it's a lot to take in," Ethan said. "They tell me you were raised in the human world."

I nodded.

Ethan gave the others a grim look before offering his hand. "Have a seat."

I followed him to a chair situated in front of the fire place that had been dormant when I arrived. Now, in the dark of night, the room was filled with the dancing glow of firelight from the hearty fire.

"I appreciate your help, all of you. And I'm sorry for the inconvenience I've caused. Perhaps you can show me to a city or a place I could find work?" I asked.

"You wouldn't last a day in the city," Cormac said.

Ethan scowled at Cormac, then turned to me. "What he means is that we think you're being hunted."

A chill ran down my spine and I hugged myself, covering the soft areas of my waist where claws had so recently dug into my flesh. I wanted to argue with him, but I had been wondering about the strange creatures that had attacked me. One attack could be a coincidence. Two was something else. "Why?"

"We don't know," Cormac said.

"We might know," Dane said.

"We don't know," Cormac repeated.

I frowned. Cormac seemed to want to hide things from me and I wasn't sure why. He didn't seem to trust me, which I supposed was fair. We didn't know each other. However, this was my life and I couldn't wait around for him. "I could use some help."

"That's true," Ethan said. "And we're going to help you."

"We haven't decided yet," Cormac said. "Ethan can do as he pleases, but Dane and I have a duty to complete."

"This is your duty, Cormac," Ethan said. "And don't forget that you called me here to help you."

"We haven't determined if she's connected yet," Cormac said.

"To hell with your determinations," Dane said. "She won't survive without us and the creatures are hunting her. We were charged with eliminating them and now we've seen them attack her twice? How could it not be connected?"

"When we first met, you told me you were hunting those things," I said. "And now you're telling me they are hunting me?"

"It seems so," Ethan said.

"It's possible," Cormac said.

"But these monsters are new?" I asked.

"We see them from time to time," Cormac said.

"We haven't seen them in a long time," Ethan said.

"And we've never seen this many at once," Dane added.

"What does it all mean?" I asked.

"That's what we were sent to find out," Dane said. "And also to kill them all." He grinned.

"So you think there's a connection between me and these beasts?" I asked, afraid to hear the answer.

"No," Cormac said.

"Yes," Dane said. "Cormac, don't deny it. They've never left

Faerie before. Two days ago, one broke free of our realm and hunted her down."

"We don't know if that's why it escaped," Cormac said.

"Stop pretending there isn't a connection," Dane said.

"The sooner we turn her in to the council, the better," Cormac said.

"What council? Someone please slow down and explain this to me," I pleaded.

"You're a changeling, which makes you council business. You shouldn't exist," Cormac said.

"We can't take her there, they'll just throw her into a random trade and if the beasts are hunting her she won't last the night," Dane said.

"You've always been soft for a pretty face," Cormac said.

"What do you mean random trade?" I asked, my spirits lifting. Wasn't that what I wanted? Freedom to take care of myself? Why would I want to turn that down?

"It isn't as bad as it sounds. You won't get a choice, but they'll help you find something you can do," Ethan said.

It didn't sound bad to me at all. I wanted a way to take care of myself now that I was on my own. Something about these Fae made me want to stay with them, but I knew that was irrational. They didn't know me and I didn't know them. The sooner I was out on my own, the better.

"And your method is better?" Cormac asked Dane, ignoring Ethan and me. "Use her as bait to hunt down the rest of the monsters?"

"At least we can protect her if we do that," Dane said.

"Stop it!" I yelled.

The three males turned to look at me. I knew I didn't want to be monster bait and I didn't want to get eaten. But worse, I didn't want to be trapped in a house with a bunch of arguing Fae. "Take me where I'm supposed to be. Please."

"Are you sure?" Ethan asked.

"I can't go home and I clearly can't stay here," I said.

"It won't be safe for you out there," Dane said.

"She'll be fine," Cormac said.

The room quieted and only the crackle of the fire punctuated the silence. I felt like I'd caused enough trouble and just wanted to find a new way of surviving in this strange place.

"Thank you for everything you've done for me." I stood and walked toward the stairs, hoping that I could find something more suitable to wear in the room upstairs. I moved slowly, giving them a chance to call me back if I were violating any social protocols I didn't know but nobody stopped me.

Just as I placed my foot on the step, a loud bang sounded behind me. I turned just as another bang cut through the air. The door buckled as the sound returned and my breath hitched as my eyes stayed focused on the front door. Something or someone was trying to break through.

Chapter Eleven

W hile I stood frozen on the stairs, the males in the room moved quickly, as if on instinct. Before I could fully comprehend what was happening, Dane had a sword drawn and Cormac was right behind him with a pair of daggers in hand.

Ethan appeared at the bottom of the steps and shoved me upward. "Go!"

I scrambled up the steps and stopped at the top before reaching the second floor, looking down just in time to see the door splinter as the all-too-familiar bat-like monster barged into the house.

I screamed and grabbed the stair rail, eyes fixed on the battle unfolding below me. I knew the creature hardly stood a chance against all three males. I'd seen them fight before and I knew they attacked ruthlessly, but that knowledge didn't prevent my lower lip from trembling as I watched.

Cormac ducked a swipe of the claws just as Dane shoved his sword into the creature's throat.

It roared, then let out large, gasping breaths that weakened into a rattling sound before the creature landed in a heap on the floor.

My shoulders dropped as I started to regain normal breathing, but the reprieve was short-lived. Two more creatures pushed their way through the door, and in a scramble of flying fabric, snapping jaws, and flashing steel, both creatures were dispatched in a bloodied mess.

My knuckles were white from gripping the stair rail so tight and my hands trembled. I waited, watching the open door to see if the attack was over. The seconds seems to drag by and I finally peeled my eyes away from the door to look down at Ethan. He was standing in front of the stairs in a ready position both arms outstretched. He'd never left his position guarding me.

My heart fluttered as warmth surged through me. Ethan had helped me when I was half naked and alone. He'd brought me here and defended me against Cormac. Now, he put himself in harm's way to keep me safe. He didn't owe me anything, in fact, I owed him, yet he defended me. I didn't even get that from the man who was supposed to be my husband.

For a moment, I wondered if Ethan was married and my cheeks heated in embarrassment. Now wasn't the time to be thinking like that. Besides, I had nothing to offer anyone here. I was penniless and destitute. It was beyond luck that I even gained the help of these males in the first place. I didn't want to think about where I'd be if I hadn't run into Cormac and Dane in the woods or if I hadn't met Ethan on the road.

In front of Ethan, both Dane and Cormac still had their weapons drawn. I owed these males everything and I didn't want to be a burden to them, but I couldn't deny that I needed their help. These monsters seemed to be following me and without them, I would be dead by morning.

"Is it over?" I asked, breaking the silence.

In front of me, Ethan lowered his arms and Dane and Cormac lowered their weapons. "You still think it's a coincidence?" Dane asked.

"Pack your things. We're leaving," Cormac said as he walked away from the open door.

A flutter of blue fabric caught my eye and I turned to see a pair of maids standing in the corner, their mouths hanging open in shock. Cormac stopped in front of them, then looked up at me before turning back to address them. "Get the girl dressed and ready for a journey."

He walked away without saying anything else and the maids curtsied after him. I was still standing frozen on the stairs when the two girls in blue dresses approached me. They both had the pointed ears characteristic of the faeries I'd met so far, but these two were smaller, slimmer, more petite than the males I'd met. They were both smaller than me. They paused two steps below me and half curtsied while balancing on the step before approaching me. "Miss, we will help you prepare for the journey."

"That's not necessary, if you just show me where things are I'm sure I can manage."

One of the maids smirked, clearly not used to having someone decline assistance. "It's no trouble, Miss."

Knowing I wasn't going to get anywhere with them, and realizing it would be silly of them to show me where things were rather than just helping, I tore myself away from the banister and climbed the stairs. In the hall, I lingered outside of the bedroom that I'd been shown to when I first arrived. "In here?"

The maids nodded and stood fixed to the floor behind me. Realizing they were probably waiting for me, I walked into the room and stood near the bed so I'd be out of the way.

I'd had maids growing up, but they tended to household duties and did things for my parents. Aside from the assistance I was given by Nani, I was used to doing things myself. My chest tightened at the thought of Nani, left behind in my rush to escape. I hoped she found her way out.

"Don't look so worried, Miss," one of the maids said. "Cormac and Dane are the best hunters in all the courts. They've never failed to stop a monster outbreak before."

I blinked a few times while I processed her words. I should have been worried about the situation right in front of me, but my thoughts were so focused on what I'd left behind.

Trying to get a hold of my thoughts, I looked at the maid. She was a petite, almost frail looking female with wispy brown hair and brown eyes that were too large for her face. Her skin was slightly blue and had the same shimmering quality the male Fae had, but she didn't seem to be the same as them. I wondered if she was something different. Were there more than just Fae or were there different types of Fae? "What's your name?"

She smiled and inclined her head. "Sari, Miss."

"You say they've hunted monsters before?" I asked.

"Of course," she said.

"Why?"

She chuckled. "It's their job, Miss. The princes have to defend their territory and protect their people. If any of the monsters from the Under find their way here, they must dispose of them and find the entrance they used so they can stop them."

"The Under?" I asked.

"Of course," she said. "Where else would the Sodalis come from?"

I wanted to ask more questions, get more details about the Sodalis, which I now knew was the name of the monster that continued to show up wherever I went. Apparently, it came from someplace called the Under. "Wait, *princes?*"

"You didn't know, Miss?" Sari asked.

I shook my head. "I'm new here."

She pressed her lips together as if stopping herself from commenting on my words. Then, her eyes softened and the smile returned. "Cormac is prince of the Autumn Court, where we are now. Dane is prince of the Summer Court, and Ethan is prince of the Spring Court."

"Don't princes usually stay in their lands?" I asked.

"Not really," she said. "They're free to travel as they wish."

"That's enough, Sari," the other maid said as she walked toward the bed. She set a pile of clothing down and turned to me. "Their business is not ours and we should not speak of it."

Before I could say anything else, she turned away from me and Sari followed her. The two of them flitted in and out of the room, adding things to the pile on the bed. Neither of them spoke to me.

Uncomfortable in the silence, I walked back toward the doorway where I found Ethan standing in the hallway. I narrowed my eyes at him. "How long have you been standing there?"

"Just a moment," he said. "I came to check on you. How are you feeling?"

"Confused, mostly," I said. "You're a prince?"

Ethan turned to look at the maids as they scurried out of my room, their eyes lowered. "I see you got to know Sari."

"Oh please don't punish her, I don't know the rules here," I said.

Ethan's brow furrowed. "Punish her? No, she's allowed to talk to you. I just know she likes to gossip. I'm surprised she didn't get your life story out of you."

"I don't understand what's going on," I said. "I don't understand this world. Where I'm from princes don't go out hunting monsters. We don't have monsters. And if we did, I can't imagine they would have any interest in chasing me."

"I'm sure this is all overwhelming," Ethan said.

"That's a mild way of putting it," I said. "I just want some answers."

"What are your questions?" he asked.

"Where do I begin?" I asked.

"Whatever comes to mind." Ethan waited patiently, a smile on his face.

I liked Ethan. He seemed genuine and warm. None of his

kindness felt forced. "Alright, what are these things? Do you really think they're chasing me? And where are we going? And why are we going there? And a hundred other questions about who you are and what this place is and how I'm going to survive."

"For now, can we just take it one question at a time?" Ethan asked.

I nodded, and found that, despite my fear and anxiety at the situation I was in, being around Ethan made me feel better. There was something calming about him that gave me hope that things might end up okay after all.

"First, the monsters. They're called Sodalis and they come from a place we refer to as the Under. It's a realm of monsters and from time to time they find their way here.

"On occasion, there's been outbreaks where large quantities of monsters escape. Most of the time, it's limited to a specific court or geographical area. This time, we've had an influx in all three courts. That's why I'm here, I came when Cormac called for me. The three of us will work together to eliminate the beasts and stop them from returning."

"So maybe it doesn't have anything to do with me?" I asked, hopeful.

"I wish that were true, but these creatures don't typically track individuals. Usually their attacks are random. The fact that you've been attacked three times now, tells us something is different this time."

I sighed, wishing there wasn't something connecting me to a bunch of bat monsters. Ethan's hand covered mine, which I had unconsciously clasped protectively over the places where I had already sustained injuries from these monsters.

Gently, Ethan moved my hand to the side and slowly lifted the fabric up from my tunic revealing my midsection and bare legs. Thankfully, whoever had changed my clothes had left my under-garments on. My breath hitched and I considered slapping him, but his concerned expression held me back.

Brow furrowed, Ethan's fingers brushed across my skin, tracing over the red marks that showed as the only remains of my injuries. His touch sent a shiver through me. I had to bite down on my lip to keep from gasping at the intensity.

"These are healing nicely," he said, dropping the tunic and lowering his hand from my waist.

I was sure my face was red in response to his touch. I was unfamiliar with any man's touch and never thought it would be something I would long for. Yet at the absence of his fingers against my skin, I found I was craving more. I wanted his bare skin against my bare skin again. Surprised to notice that my breathing had grown shallow, I turned away from Ethan to collect myself. So this was what attraction felt like.

"I'm glad you healed quickly," Ethan said. "It's not a gift that every Fae has."

Grateful that he either didn't notice or didn't acknowledge my behavior, I turned back to him. "It's not?"

I had credited my quick healing with the fact that I wasn't human. If it wasn't something that every Fae had, I suppose I was incredibly lucky given my current circumstance. "Is it true then, all faeries have magic?"

"Yes, that's true. That's an easy question." Ethan chuckled.

"So what does that mean? If I have healing magic?"

"Each of us is born into a different realm. I'm Spring. One of the things that usually come with being a Spring Fae is a gift for healing. We also have a gift for life. We excel at helping things grow and heal."

"Does that mean whoever abandoned me was a Spring Fae?" I asked.

He shrugged. "Perhaps they were from the Spring Court. But I don't think they abandoned you. It's not easy to arrange for a baby to be swapped like you were. There was planning and time invested in your placement along with money."

I straightened as I recalled the secret conversation my father was having before I escaped. "My father said someone was paying him and the family I was supposed to marry into to keep me hidden. Do you think whoever was paying them might be the one who sent me away?"

"Maybe," he said. "If someone wanted to harm you or keep you away from Faerie for good, they could have killed you. Instead, they were doing whatever they could to keep you trapped in the mortal world."

"But that doesn't explain the monster attacks," I said.

"No, I don't think the two things are related. It's rare, but there are a few other times a creature from the Under has found its way to the mortal realm. It just hasn't happened in hundreds of years. Honestly, you're just lucky it was a Sodalis and not something worse."

"What could possibly be worse?" I shivered as I recalled the dripping saliva and sharp claws of the beast.

"Trust me," he said. "You don't want to know."

Chapter Twelve

Cormac appeared in the doorway. "Are you ready?"

I stared at him and tried to think of something witty to say. I didn't get the sense that Cormac enjoyed my presence, I felt like an inconvenience.

"She's ready for changing into riding clothes, your grace," the maid said.

"I'll leave you to it then," Cormac said before he walked away.

"Is he always like that?" I asked Ethan.

"Don't worry about him," Ethan said. "Pretty sure he wouldn't know what fun was if it jumped up and bit him."

"Right this way, Miss. We'll help you prepare," Sari said, waving me back into the room.

I was ushered away by the maids before I got to say goodbye to Ethan. As I stood there, the two females stripped my clothing and helped me into leather trousers and a thick wool tunic. As they laced, tied, and fastened me, I couldn't help but think about Ethan. "Can you tell me more about the Spring prince?" I asked.

"I don't know much about him, Miss," Sari said. "We see him around from time to time, but he stays fairly private. I don't think he's found a mate, if that's what you are asking."

"Sari!" the other maid said.

I wanted to ask her name, but she didn't seem like she wanted to get to know me. I wasn't sure why that was and I wondered if it had anything to do with her master. "What about Cormac?"

"He's fair, and wise, and kind. Nothing like his father," Sari said.

"That is quite enough," the second maid said. She shoved me down onto a chair and went to work on my hair, brushing out the tangles and working the knots of the last few days free.

Given that I was about to go on a journey for who knew how long, I would have liked for nothing more than to have a proper bath one last time before hitting a dusty road. One that wasn't in a freezing stream. I had a feeling if I asked for that now, Cormac might just haul me out naked and throw me on a horse without waiting.

He seemed to be in a rush, and I couldn't blame him. I wasn't particularly keen to have the monsters reappear at his doorstep.

"So are there kings?" I asked. "Is Cormac's father the king?"

"Of course there are kings," Sari said. "There just aren't kings of the individual courts. Cormac's father is the Autumn Minister. He's the queen's right hand and oversees this court for her."

"So there are three courts? Autumn, Spring, and Summer? What about Winter?" I asked.

"We do not speak of Winter," Sari said, voice serious for the first time. "There are three courts, ruled and governed by a fair queen. She has consorts, known as Kings. She rules above all the courts and the Ministers and princes oversee their individual courts at her behest."

After several minutes of yanking and tugging, I had to assume that my hair was in some sort of satisfactory state. But the grumpy maid continued to work her way through my blonde curls. I wondered what she was doing.

I looked up toward the doorway to see Dane leaning against the doorframe. His head was cocked to the side and he wore a smirk. *Maybe*, I thought, *he finds the entire situation funny.* My hair was probably in a wild mane after all the brushing. Dry curls and a hairbrush didn't mix but I wasn't about to tell that to the grumpy maid.

"How long have you been watching me?" I asked. "It is typical for you? Lurking in doorways and staring at women?"

"I can't say I've had the pleasure of lurking before," he said. He dropped his folded arms to his side and strolled over to me. "I'm not sure what it is with you, but you sure seem to find a way to anger not only the monsters but also Cormac. I've never seen him quite so undone by a female. It's possible he might like you," he said.

"If the behavior he's been showing me is what he does when he likes someone, he must not have many friends."

"You have much to learn," Dane said. "Jehle, you almost done with her hair? She's going to be traveling by horseback, not going to a ball."

The maid I now knew was called Jehle, lifted her hands from my head immediately. "I'm sorry, sir, she's finished."

"Always so serious, Jehle." Dane winked at Jehle. "That must be why you're Cormac's favorite."

I thought I actually saw a smile on Jehle's lips, but it was so fleeting it was difficult to tell. She curtsied and turned away from Dane, then returned with a bag in her hand. "This is all we could find. His grace didn't have much that's suitable for a lady anymore."

"I'm sure it's sufficient," Dane took the bag then inclined his head, "thank you, Jehle."

Dane offered his hand to me. "Cormac's waiting, you ready?"

"I don't even know what we're doing, but if the maid says I'm ready, I suppose I am," I said.

"You look beautiful. I'd say you're ready," Dane said.

"Thanks," I said, taking the offered hand.

"We're riding to see an old friend of Cormac's," Dane said as we walked toward the staircase. "After that, we'll see what happens. And don't worry, one way or another, we'll make sure you learn about being Fae."

"Thank you." That was the most reassuring thing I'd heard since I arrived. I didn't want to be an inconvenience, but the amount of things I didn't know was staggering.

Before I could stop myself, I reached up to feel my ear, noting the pointed end that had appeared after the monster attacked. It was strange having a part of your body one way your whole life and then suddenly find that it was never meant to be that way.

I wondered if that was how it would feel about everything here. Would it feel more natural than the human realm eventually? Or would I always feel like a stranger here?

In some ways, I always felt like a stranger while growing up. I wanted such different things than my sister. My mother and I never quite understood why. I thought I just had an adventurous spirit, it turned out I was never human.

"You'll get used to things," Dane said. "And we'll help you until you figure it out."

"That's not what it sounds like according to Cormac," I said. "Honestly, I'm not sure I could handle being left somewhere. I'm just starting to figure all of this out. Apparently I have magic and nothing is what I thought it was."

"I think that's why they outlawed changelings in the first place. Most changelings would eventually find their way back here and it's a difficult period of adjustment to go from the human world to our world."

"What happened to them?" I asked. "The other changelings?"

Dane didn't answer. Instead, he descended the stairs as if he had never heard me. I hurried to catch him and grabbed his tunic when we reached the bottom of the steps, pulling him closer to me.

"What happened to the other changelings?" I stared into his blue eyes and tried not to get sucked into his good looks and charm. Despite his easy personality, there was something dangerous about those eyes. Something that threatened to pull me in and never let me go.

All of these princes came across as males who weren't challenged often, which I supposed made sense since they were royalty. I wasn't sure what made me so willing to challenge them. Perhaps I didn't know any better or perhaps confusion and fear of this place were greater than the fear of these males.

Dane's expression was stern, his jaw tight. I didn't break the gaze and kept my eyes focused on him. "What's the real reason it's illegal? What happened to the other changelings?"

Dane sighed, his jaw softened. For a moment his expression looked like pity before returning to his usual easy smile. "Changelings aren't allowed. Many of the great houses use to try to hide some of their children and bring them back here as bargaining chips or late entries into the Queen's Trial. It was always a gamble and sometimes had short-term gain, but none of those hidden children ever survived."

"None? No changeling has ever survived after coming back here? What happens to them?" Ignoring all of the other implications of this statement, the court drama that seemed to be no different than that of the human world and some event called 'Queen's Trial', I focused on the lack of surviving changelings.

"Time to go," Cormac's voice carried up the stairs.

"Later," Dane said. "Now it's time to go."

Chapter Thirteen

The sky was painted in orange and pink and the sun peeked out from the horizon as we walked from the house to the stables. I'd slept through the night, but not as long as I imagined I had. Thankfully, I was finally starting to feel like my energy had returned.

"You think Angela is going to be happy to see you?" Ethan asked.

"How long has it been? Twenty years? Fifty?" Dane asked.

"Not long enough," Ethan mumbled under his breath.

I was surprised to hear him say something negative about someone. Ethan seemed to like everyone. Whoever Angela was, she must have done something terrible.

"I still don't understand why we have to go see her," Dane said.

"She's neutral," Cormac said. "And she might be able to explain why the creatures are after Cassia."

"So you admit it!" Dane said triumphantly.

Cormac glared at him.

"So who is this Angela, anyway?" I asked.

"Cormac's former mate," Ethan said.

"Angela is not really something that can be described," Dane said. "She is something you have to experience."

"That's enough," Cormac said.

"You know one of these days, I'd like to start understanding the things that are happening around me," I said.

"That's probably how Cormac feels about you," Dane said.

Cormac ignored the jest as he helped me onto my horse. "Do you know how to ride?"

I grabbed a hold of the reins and positioned myself better in the saddle. "I bet I can ride circles around you."

Cormac smirked. The first time I honestly saw any flicker of positive emotion from him. It was a bit startling. "Well, this isn't a race. But if we were racing, I doubt you could keep up with me."

"That sounds like a challenge," I said.

Cormac mounted his own horse and turned back to look at me. "Maybe one day we'll test that out. But for now, just try to keep up." He clicked his tongue and pulled on the reins, starting off down the dirt road faster than necessary.

I smiled and pulled back on the reins letting the gray and white mare know that it was time to follow.

The rush of the wind in my hair and the bite of the chill on my cheeks made me feel more alive than I had in days. This was my happy place. I was comfortable here. I knew how to do this. Riding was safe and familiar.

I liked horses more than I liked most people. I'd always felt an easy affinity with animals and they seemed to feel the same toward me. I'd yet to meet an animal I couldn't charm. This horse was no exception. The two of us got into an easy rhythm, instantly finding comfort in the other. She didn't feel like a new horse to me, she felt as familiar to me as my horse at home, the one that I had raised from a pony.

I kept my eyes on Cormac as we traveled in a cloud of dust along the dirt road. I knew Ethan and Dane were right behind us, but it was hard to focus on anything other than the feeling of freedom that speeding down this road gave me. For the first time since weeks before my wedding, I felt the pressure in my chest lift and I felt peace and wholeness roll through me.

I took a deep breath, filling my nose with the scent of wood smoke and pine. Buried in there, was also the scent of fresh, damp earth. A rainbow of red and gold and deep purple passed by us as we rode. With each passing moment, my discomfort seemed to ease. When I'd first arrived, everything felt so foreign. As I felt the rush of the wind in my hair and felt the freedom of riding through the country, I let the fear wash away from me.

There might be bat beasts trying to catch me, but there was a peace in this place that I hadn't noticed before. It was different than the human world. There was something more pure about this place. Suddenly, I felt like I belonged here, I belonged with the other Fae in this realm.

The human world was a place of constant anxiety and fear. I worried all the time about every little thing. I had always thought it was just because I was so different from my family and then I thought all of my anxiety stemmed from my upcoming marriage. The only place I had ever felt comfortable and free, was when I was riding my horse. But I had never felt the way I felt now. Was this what life was supposed to be?

Cormac slowed and I rode up alongside him, slowing my horse to match his pace. He turned and looked at me, another smile on his face. My heart fluttered in response. He was a very handsome male, especially when he smiled. All of the grumpiness and seriousness had prevented me from seeing just how attractive he really was.

"You are a good rider," he said, sounding surprised.

"Was that a compliment?" I asked.

"I can give compliments," he said.

"You also know how to smile," I said.

He laughed. It was a deep, rich sound and it sent a thrill all the way to my toes. Did he know how handsome he was? For a moment, I had a strange flicker of jealousy as I realized we were going to see his old girlfriend. That didn't make any sense so I pushed the thought away and smiled back at Cormac. It seemed horseback riding was his happy place too.

"You like animals." It wasn't a question, for some reason I could tell it wasn't just horses that made Cormac happy. He seemed like he was more at peace when he was outdoors like maybe he needed to be around nature. Perhaps he was like me in that sense, more comfortable around animals than other people. Or in his case, more comfortable around animals than other Fae.

"We understand each other," he said. "A lot of us in the Autumn Court have a unique affinity with animals. We connect with them on a deeper level."

"Is that part of your magic then?" I asked.

"I suppose it is. We have this sense with creatures where it's easier to know how they're feeling, what they're thinking, or what they might do. It's part of why I'm tasked with finding monsters when they break through. Those with this gift have an affinity for tracking. I can better anticipate what an animal might do."

"I've always felt more comfortable around animals than people," I said.

"Perhaps you hail from the Autumn Court," he said.

Before I could comment or ask questions further, Cormac halted his horse's progress and my horse followed suit.

I tore my eyes off of him to look ahead of us and found that we were outside a small cottage.

"We're here." Cormac dismounted and led his horse over to a small fence post that stood in the middle of nowhere. It wasn't a continuing fence, so it looked like it had been built just for this purpose. I dismounted, and followed Cormac over to the post to tie my own horse.

"What happened to not racing?" Ethan asked.

"I thought you two were going to take off and leave us," Dane said.

Both Dane and Ethan appeared to be breathing a little heavy. Maybe Cormac and I had been going faster than I thought.

Cormac was already at the front door, leaving me alone with Ethan and Dane. Neither of them moved toward the post to tie their horses and I wondered what they were waiting for.

"Do either of you have an affinity with animals?" I asked.

"Oh no, that's more of an Autumn Court thing," Ethan said.

I knew Ethan had healing magic as part of his Spring Court bloodline and now I knew Cormac had an affinity with animals. "Where are you from, Dane?"

"Summer Court," he said.

"And what is a Summer Court known for?" I asked.

"Heat," he said.

"Heat?" I asked.

"All kinds of heat," Dane winked.

"Really, Dane?" Ethan said.

"What can I say? Us Summer Court Fae are known to be the best lovers in all the courts. I'm not going to pretend that's not part of the magic we were given."

"I don't think that's what she was asking about, Dane," Ethan said.

My lower body was tingling in a fashion I wasn't used to. Part of me wanted to know more about what made the Summer Court have a reputation for being the best lovers. But that wasn't something I was about to ask. Though, I had a feeling they knew what I was thinking because I could feel the heat rising to my cheeks. Knowing my blush would give me away, I turned away from the two of them and walked toward Cormac who was waiting at the front door.

"We'll wait out here," Ethan said from behind us.

I turned to look at him, confused as to why he would stay outside. Then I looked back at Cormac. "Should I go in?"

"Of course you're going in. We are here for you after all."

Chapter Fourteen

So the seriousness has returned. Cormac knocked gently on
the door and my insides twisted in anticipation as I waited
to see who would greet us. For some reason, I pictured a tall dark-
haired woman with long legs in a dress with a plunging neckline.
Whoever this woman was, in order to have such a hold on
Cormac, she must be stunning.

The door opened but no one was standing there to greet us.
Beyond the doorway, I was surprised to see how dark the interior
of the home was. Cormac pushed the door open the rest of the
way and swept his arm toward the entryway indicating that I
should enter.

Hesitantly, I stepped into the darkened space. Once inside,
Cormac followed me then shut the door behind us. I looked
around the little cabin we had entered. It was much larger on the
inside than I had anticipated.

The whole space was as dark as if it were nighttime, but it was
lit with floating candles above me that flickered like starlight in
the night sky. Despite the darkness, the candlelight gave the place
a comforting warm glow and I found my tension easing now that
we were inside.

Whoever lived there must like soft lighting and drama. The floor was rustic wood, clean and soft, but missing the high-gloss polish of Cormac's estate. This place was much homier and simpler.

The walls were bare wood and free of decoration. In front of us, was a small fireplace with a humble fire burning in the hearth. A countertop with a pitcher and a few stools probably served as both work area and dining table.

The only thing in the room that looked like it may have been expensive, were four large overstuffed chairs arranged in a half-circle in front of the fireplace. The only other things in the small space were two closed doors.

I wondered if they both led to bedrooms or if whoever lived there had upgraded the cabin enough to have an inside bathroom. As I was staring at them, one of the doors opened and a tall, slender Fae female with dark brown hair emerged. She was indeed wearing a dress with a very low neckline and looked like she had very long legs. My brow furrowed as I realized she looked exactly as I imagined she would.

The woman glided across the floor, her light brown dress grazing the wood as she walked toward one of the plush chairs. "Well, are you going to sit or you going to make me wait all day?" She settled into one of the chairs.

Cormac took the seat next to her and I took the chair across from her. She looked up at me and I realized that her eyes were milky white. I let out a gasp before I could stop myself then covered my mouth feeling bad for my rudeness.

"Yes, I'm blind," she said. "Traded one kind of sight for another. Funny how the fates work."

In the village I'd grown up in, one of the children I used to play with had a blind grandfather. It was amazing the things the man could do without the gift of sight, yet I always felt unsure of how to act around him. Even after years of spending time around him, I still hesitated every time I saw him.

"It's okay, I don't bite," Angela said.

"I apologize for my rudeness," I said.

"I get it. What I'm more interested in is the fact that you knew what I looked like before you even met me. Is that a typical occurrence for you?" she asked.

I could feel Cormac's gaze on me, but I didn't turn toward him for fear of what I would see on his face. Angela's words were so accusatory I was worried I had done something wrong. My pulse rose and a trickle of fear slid down my back. "I don't know how I did that. I've never done it before."

"Why did you bring her here today, Cormac?" Angela asked.

"She's a changeling. We found her being attacked by a Sodalis in the mortal world. And the creatures seem to be drawn to her," he said.

"Changeling. Well, that explains the human smell of you," she said.

"Human smell?" I asked.

"If you ever make it back to the human world, you'll notice. I'm sure you feel much more comfortable now that you're here. More at peace, am I correct?" she asked.

Yesterday I would have answered that question differently, but something seemed to have changed for me today. "Yes."

"Do you know where you came from?" she asked. "Sometimes changeling children are left with trinkets or mementos, something we can use to trace them back to their family. Were you left with any such thing?"

"If I was, it's long gone," I said.

"You do realize that if you have seer blood it could mean one of your parents was from the Winter Court," she said.

"I didn't realize that. In fact, I don't know anything about any of this. It's all brand-new to me."

"You really think a family from the Winter Court would have risked hiding a child in the human world?" Cormac asked.

"I thought we weren't supposed to talk about the Winter Court," I said.

"Aye, so it is that you know some things," Angela said.

"I suppose I am picking up a few things here and there," I said.

"I'm not here about her lineage," Cormac said.

I was curious about my lineage and very curious about where I belonged. So far, it seemed I could belong anywhere. I wondered if that meant that I belonged nowhere. It was bad enough that I'd been hidden away by parents who either didn't want me or felt I was in such great danger they had to hide me. I already felt confused enough about who I was without adding in the element of which court I hailed from. "Does it matter where I came from?"

"It does if you want to learn how to use your magic. But that will come in time," Angela said. "So if you're not here about finding her family, you're here because of the Sodalis."

"I was hoping maybe she could stay with you while we hunted them. They seem to be especially drawn to her and I'm not sure why," Cormac said.

I looked over at Cormac, unable to hide the shock in my expression. I didn't know we were here so he could dump me off on someone else.

"She can't stay here," Angela said.

Relief flooded through me. Angela seemed nice enough, but I wasn't particularly keen on the idea of staying for an unknown amount of time in a stranger's tiny cabin. Plus, there was something unsettling about Angela that had nothing to do with her eyes. Something about her made me uncomfortable.

"Those creatures are going to keep coming after her until you seal the opening they broke free from," Angela said. "And if you leave her here, they'll all start tracking her here. You may even find they make more tears in the Under. That will make your job much more difficult."

I frowned. The way she spoke was so logical and detached. She didn't seem to mind that the creatures might harm me.

"Have you seen something?" Cormac asked.

"I've seen lots of things. But there is something that greatly concerns me. As you know, my visions are constantly shifting, we never know if they'll actually come to pass. However, there's been a reoccurring vision lately and I worry that if you don't get these bat beasts under control, this vision will become reality."

"What did you see?" Cormac asked.

"I see all four courts falling at the hands of monsters that have not been in our lands since before the time of the Queens. I see so many tears between our realm and that of the Under that they cannot possibly ever be contained. I see monsters flooding out of Faerie and into the human realm en masse. I see darkness and death and decay."

Icy cold fear spread down my chest into my fingertips and down to my toes. Her words were terrifying and as the wheels spun in my mind, I connected the dots. If magic was real, there was no reason to doubt that this woman could see the future. "I don't understand what this has to do with me."

"You have something the beasts want. Something attracting them. And they're not going to stop until they get it."

"Is sealing the tear enough? Is there anything else we have to do?" Cormac asked.

"With this vision, I don't know what the cause is. But I do know if those creatures are hunting her, they will continue to do so until they have her. You have to seal the tear or more are going to come out. The word is out about your girl and more will come until she's gone."

She looked over at me and it sent a shiver down my spine. Her lifeless eyes seemed to stare a hole into my soul, as if she could read all of my thoughts, my dreams, and my fears.

"I suppose you could sacrifice her now. That might be the

easiest and most efficient way to prevent an infestation." Angela shrugged.

"I'm not taking an innocent life," Cormac said. "Give me something else. Something that will help."

I held my breath and gritted my teeth as I tried to swallow back the anger and disgust that had risen into my throat at Angela's cavalier suggestion that Cormac sacrifice me for the greater good. I had no intention of dying. Especially now that I finally found a place where I felt like I belonged. I needed to explore this realm more; find out all of the things that made me unique; find out how my magic worked. And maybe even find out where I came from.

"If you take her with you, it will make the tracking easier. And if she lives through this, I'd say the gods will it."

Angela stood, then Cormac stood as well. I pushed myself to standing and followed Cormac's lead.

"There's no other way?" Cormac asked.

I frowned. Cormac didn't want to kill me, which was a good thing. But he still saw me as an inconvenience. I needed to change that. "I can help. You know I know how to ride and I can help you track these things."

Angela smirked. "Aye, that she can. I can sense that in her. With a little guidance, I daresay she could match your skill level."

Now Angela had gone from suggesting Cormac kill me to suggesting Cormac teach me. While I still hadn't forgiven her for the original suggestion, her new idea was a major improvement. "See? I'm a fast learner."

Cormac grumbled under his breath, but I couldn't make out the words. Then he turned toward the door and in two large steps he was at the doorknob. He pulled it open, and turned back to Angela. "It's always a pleasure, Angela."

"Likewise, love." Angela turned and walked away from us without even waiting for us to leave.

I wondered if this was customary of how the Fae behaved or if this was just Angela.

"Cassia." Cormac lifted his chin toward the door.

I followed the silent instruction, relieved to be leaving the cabin. Now I understood why Dane and Ethan wanted to wait outside.

Aside from the way she spoke about me as if I were nothing of importance, Angela left you feeling a bit empty and confused. I couldn't have imagined staying in her house by myself for any amount of time.

As we walked back toward the horses I couldn't help but feel that flip of jealousy again at the idea of Cormac ever being in relationship with that woman. "You and Angela?"

"It was a long time ago," Cormac said. Then he busied himself preparing the horses, clearly not willing to engage in further conversation.

"So I take it that means Cassia is not staying with Angela?" Ethan asked.

"She's going to ride with us. We'll teach her to track, maybe even teach her to hunt or fight." Cormac mounted his horse and looked down at the rest of us. "Are you coming?"

I pulled myself up into my saddle wanting to show that I could do this without help. Cormac lifted his eyebrow and I swore I saw the faintest hint of a smile on his lips. Without another word from him, he took off, and the rest of us followed behind him.

Chapter Fifteen

C ormac stayed just ahead of us as we continued to ride down what seemed to be the only road in the Autumn Court. As we rode, I wondered how much longer we'd have to go before we ran into any other signs of life. We were going too fast for me to notice the details in the trees, but even if I could just catch a glimpse of a chipmunk or a deer or a squirrel, I would feel much better.

I was surprised the horses could sustain this pace for so long. I was starting to get sore from the ride, but I would never admit that to Cormac. Finally, after what felt like hours in the saddle, he slowed and I caught up to him. Ahead, was the first fork in the road we'd encountered since we began this journey. To the right, I saw signs of life and made a happy choking sound as I subconsciously turned my mount toward civilization.

"Wait here," Cormac said, halting his progress.

I stopped next to him and turned to look for Dane and Ethan. They were surprisingly far behind us and I wondered if it was a strategy they planned for or if Cormac and I were riding that much faster than them. When they joined us at the fork in the road, they slowed to a stop.

"This is the last town we'll pass through today so we might as well stop at the Inn," Cormac said.

"Perfect," said Dane. "We should make it just in time for supper."

"Always thinking with your stomach," Ethan said.

"Better than thinking with something else," said Cormac.

I turned to look at him. "Was that a joke?"

"An inappropriate one at that," said Dane.

"Let's go," Cormac said.

I stifled a giggle before pulling back on the reins to follow him. It seemed the more time we spent together, the more glimpses of each male's personality came through. They were all so different and I couldn't help but want to get to know each of them better.

In a way, maybe it was a good thing I was stuck on this trip with them. After all, once they sent me to wherever it was I was going to have to go, I wasn't sure how quickly I'd find companionship. Nobody knew me here and the idea of being alone wasn't as appealing as it had been in the beginning. I was in such a rush to get away from my father and the marriage that was being paid for by someone I didn't know, that I hadn't stopped to think about how sad it might be to be by myself, starting over in a new place.

We rode slowly through town, single file down the road. It wasn't much of a town, but it was civilization, which made me happy. Small buildings with storefronts lined the road and as we continued on I saw a crowd gathered ahead of us in what appeared to be a town square.

Cormac stopped his horse and dismounted as we approached the group. I wasn't sure if the tangle of emotions I was feeling was excitement or fear. This was going to be the first time I saw the Fae who lived in Faerie aside from my three male escorts and their servants. I wondered if they looked just like Cormac, Dane, and Ethan. Was everyone who lived here absurdly attractive?

Would I see women and children and short Fae and fat Fae and Fae with varying skin colors like I saw at home?

I dismounted and cautiously followed Cormac who wasn't slowing as we approached the group. Clearly, he wasn't concerned about the Fae ahead of us. That helped me ease the emotions inside me away from fear and more toward excitement.

Music filled the air as we drew nearer and I could hear the din of the crowd punctuated with laughter and cheering. Someone noticed our approach and left the gathering to walk toward us. He was in a hunter green tunic and gray leggings, wearing a wide smile with very flushed cheeks. He swayed a little as he walked, a sign that he had been drinking far too much.

As he drew nearer, I noticed the same pointed ears as the other Fae males, though this male didn't have the same chiseled features and good looks that my companions had. He was softer, his face was round and his body was round to match. This was a man who liked his luxury items. He clearly liked to drink and I was sure he liked to eat. He was comfortable and well cared for, likely a man of means who never had to struggle to worry about where his next meal came from.

He stopped when he reached Cormac and the silly grin on his face melted into a more serious expression. He swept his arms wide, bowing low and pausing for a moment before righting himself again. "Your grace, we didn't expect to see you here. We are honored by your presence."

"We're passing through and hoping to stay for the night," Cormac said. "We did not mean to intrude."

"I'm afraid all the rooms are booked at the inn, your grace," the man said. "But if you would be willing to do me the honor, you're welcome to stay at my estate. I'm Nikolai, the mayor of this town. And today is my daughter's wedding."

I tensed, not eager to be participating or witnessing anything that had to do with a wedding anytime soon.

"There are four of us, sir. Do you have room for us all?" Cormac asked.

"Yes," Nikolai said. "You and your lady can take my chambers for the evening and we have guest rooms for your friends."

I coughed as I tried to cover the laugh at the idea of being Cormac's lady. It wasn't that I didn't find him attractive, the opposite was true in fact. I found him incredibly attractive and at the mention of sharing a room with him I found myself picturing what he might look like without his clothes on. The notion frightened me, especially after how accurate the vision of Angela had been prior to seeing her. I squeezed my eyes shut and tried to change my focus, moving away from what I was sure was a very accurate representation of a chiseled chest, washboard abs and a perfectly shaped rear end.

"That's very kind of you, but unnecessary. The four of us can stay in your visitor's quarters."

"And would you gentlemen and lady care to join us in the festivities?" Nikolai asked.

The last thing I wanted to do was sit at someone else's wedding. But before I could object, Cormac nodded. "That would be very agreeable. Thank you for the invitation."

"It is our honor to have you here."

Nikolai clapped his hands and from out of nowhere appeared two smaller Fae males with the same small build as the maids at Cormac's house. Despite the fact that Nikolai was only barely taller than me, these two only came to his shoulders. If it weren't for the look in their eyes and their hardened expressions I would have mistaken them for children. They were dressed in matching blue tunics with tan leggings. The blue of their tunic was the same color as the blue of the dresses worn by the maids. It seemed in the Autumn Court, servants had a dress code. The two smaller males bowed in greeting when they approached us.

"Please see to these horses, you can get them settled in my personal stables," Nikolai said.

The two servants walked forward and took hold of the reins from Cormac and waited for me to hand over mine. I hesitated for a moment, not quite ready to part with the horse that represented my freedom. On foot in a strange land, I couldn't get very far. With a horse I had possibilities.

"It's all right, they'll care for her," Cormac said.

I let go of the reins, but I still didn't feel good about it. I gently stroked the side of the horse and leaned into her. I almost felt as close to her as I had to my horse growing up. "See you soon," I whispered.

Feeling sheepish, I backed away as one of the servants led our horses away.

"I know how you feel," Cormac said. "She is a special horse."

"I never got her name," I said.

"We call her Starlight. The night she was born there was a meteor shower."

"It's a beautiful name. And she's a beautiful horse," I said.

"She's really taking a liking to you," Cormac said. "You can take her with you when you go your own way."

"That's far too generous," I said even as my heart swelled at the thought of having my very own horse again.

"Think nothing of it." Cormac turned away from me, his signal that our conversation was over.

I turned away from him and stared out at the festivities in front of us. People were dancing and passing around giant goblets which I had to assume were full of wine.

The music was cheerful, played by a group of musicians near the center of the crowd. I recognized the sound of the flute and the sound of a fiddle, but some of the other instruments were foreign to me.

Cormac took a few steps away from me then turned back. "You should go and find something to entertain yourself." Then he turned away again and disappeared into the crowd.

"We'll probably be hauling him back to the place drunk off his ass tonight," Dane said. "He's never been good at weddings."

"I'm surprised he agreed to stay," Ethan said.

"What about you two?" I asked, not wanting to get into my own dislike of weddings.

"Oh, I love weddings," Dane said. "Always full of the most beautiful females."

"You're a cad, you know that?" Ethan said.

"Oh, I know that. If you'll excuse me, there is a redhead I just have to meet." Dane walked away leaving Ethan and me the sole remaining members of our group standing on the outskirts of the party.

"I'm sure you didn't expect to find yourself at a wedding this soon," Ethan said.

"To be honest, I really didn't expect to see myself at a wedding ever again."

"I'm sure you'll change your mind eventually. For now," Ethan extended his hand, "how about a dance?"

Chapter Sixteen

I wasn't in a dancing mood but Ethan's smile and sparkling blue eyes had a way of softening my resolve. I couldn't help but reach out and take his hand.

Before I knew what was happening, I was dragged into the middle of the festivities and Ethan spun me and twisted me and pulled me across the dance floor.

He moved with graceful ease and I practically tripped over my toes trying to keep up with him. The movements were unfamiliar, but the music was glorious. It filled me with joy and excitement that chipped away at my discomfort. It seemed to send my own traumatic wedding to the back of my memories where I hoped it would stay buried.

Ethan dragged me to a circle of partygoers who were clapping their hands in unison. In time with the song, the members of the circle started to move. Ethan positioned us in place, following along with the others.

First, all the men stepped into the center of the ring and turned to face their female partners. I giggled and Ethan bowed low and exaggerated. Then he rose, and extended both hands. I glanced to the side and noticed that the girls next to me were taking the hands of their male partners. I followed their example and held on to him. Next thing I knew, we were spinning until I was in the center of the circle.

The woman next to me dropped her partner's hands and curtsied low. Trying to keep up as best I could, I followed her example. I curtsied, then rose to face Ethan. His face radiated pure joy and his eyes sparkled with happiness. Dancing was clearly his happy place. It filled my heart with joy to know that I could join in.

Ethan turned sideways along with the other males and bent his elbow. The females threaded their arms through the elbows of their partner. Once we were locked elbow to elbow, the circle began to move. I laughed as I ran around with all the dancers, Ethan at my side.

The music changed tone and the dancers repositioned themselves at the starting point again. This time, I didn't have to watch the movements and I let myself get lost in the dance. By the time the song was over, I was sweating and laughing so hard I no longer cared that we were at a wedding.

Somewhere nearby, someone had started a bonfire and the music changed from the playful dancing songs to a more melancholy, reserved tune. The circle of dancers had dissipated and people wandered toward one of three large tables that were spread with plates and silverware and goblets and piled high with food.

Taking me by the hand, Ethan led me to one of the tables. When everyone was seated, a couple stood where we had all been dancing before. The female wore an ivory dress trimmed in silver and gold. Her long, flowing brown hair was woven with ribbons and flowers. Her cheeks were flushed pink with excitement and her brown eyes sparkled with what looked like pure happiness.

Her husband stood a few inches taller than her and wore his dark hair and tight curls cropped close to his head. His gray and black tunic was trimmed in the same silver and gold pattern as his bride's dress. And just like her, his pink cheeks, wide eyes and huge grin showed the whole world how happy they were to be here together.

I wondered if this was an arranged marriage and the two were just lucky or if they were allowed to marry for love. The music changed again, into a beautiful song that was unmistakably a love ballad.

The two held each other close and danced slowly while the partygoers watched. Occasionally, someone would release a heavy sigh or an affectionate sound. It was a sweet, almost intimate moment and it seemed strange to be witnessing it. There was something beautiful and fulfilling about seeing this couple share their love like this.

At the end of the song, the couple let go of each other and turned back to the crowd. Everyone rose from their seats, clapping and shouting. The father of the bride ran to greet the couple with two goblets in his hand. He handed one to each of them and then returned to his table where he lifted his own glass. Everyone around us grabbed their goblet and raised it. I reached for my own and lifted it into the air, feeling festive and happy. Maybe coming to this wedding was a good thing for me. It was nice to see that love and happiness were things that existed here in Faerie.

"To Mia and Samson, blessings of love, prosperity, and happiness," Nikolai said before taking a drink of his goblet.

The couple joined in, taking a drink of their own. From somewhere behind me, someone shouted, "And lots of little babies!"

Everyone laughed and the couple's pink cheeks turned a deeper shade of red. The two of them ran back to the center table sitting down in spaces that had been reserved for them. Then everyone started passing around food and chatting with their neighbors.

It was a festive and cheerful mood and it was easy to relax and enjoy the delicious food. But as I sat there eating while Ethan was deep in conversation with the person across the table from him, I couldn't help but wonder how Cormac was doing. The others seemed fine, excited even at the prospect of attending this event. Cormac had stormed off on his own and I hadn't seen him since.

I glanced around, and quickly found Dane with the redhead on his lap. He was clearly enjoying himself. I had nothing to worry about other than him potentially breaking someone's heart. I tried to tell myself that wasn't my business, though I felt a little bit bad for her and a little bit jealous of her. That was something I needed to stop doing, I didn't have a claim on any of the Fae males I was traveling with. They were helping me while they hunted escaped monsters. And I knew that as soon as they completed their task, they would send me away.

The thought saddened me so I pushed it away, not wanting to think about it tonight. I excused myself from the table, but Ethan was so engaged in his conversation he didn't seem to notice. I was glad he was having a good time, but I was still worried about Cormac. I knew he could take care of himself, but I'd feel better if I found him. I walked past the other tables, scanning them for any sight of the dark haired prince. He didn't appear to be among any of the guests who were seated at the tables. The center square where we had danced was now abandoned. Even the instruments were sitting without the musicians. On the other side of the tables was the bonfire where one solitary figure was standing silhouetted against the flames.

I glanced back at Ethan and Dane before I walked away from where I was standing near the tables. Both of them were engaged in conversation. Figuring they wouldn't miss me, I walked carefully and slowly toward the lone figure by the bonfire. As I grew nearer, it was clear that my guess had been correct.

Cormac stood there staring into the fire, bottle of wine in his hand. He lifted the bottle and took a long pull before lowering it again. I couldn't see his face yet, but he seemed fixated on that fire.

I paused before I got too close and considered turning back. He looked like he wanted to be alone and I wasn't sure if I should interrupt.

"I'm not good company right now," he said.

I took his words as an invitation and I moved closer. I stopped right next to him, keeping my eyes on the dancing flames in front of us. "They say it's bad luck to be alone at a wedding," I said.

I heard him swallow and turned in time to see him wiping his mouth with the back of his hand. "As far as I'm concerned, everything about weddings is bad luck."

"Then why did you agree to come?" I asked.

"It would reflect poorly on me as prince of this land to turn down the invitation. Especially when getting a favor from the host," he said.

I glanced down at the bottle he was holding then reached for it, pulling it from his grasp. He opened his mouth as if he wanted to object, but as soon as I put the bottle to my lips he closed his mouth. The liquid was sweet and burned my throat on its way down. I winced and handed him the bottle back.

"It's mead." He took another pull of the bottle.

The sweet taste lingered on my tongue. I could feel the liquid coating the inside of my mouth. I'd never had mead before. I knew the villagers where I grew up made it from time to time.

Intrigued, I reached for the bottle again and took another swig before passing it back to Cormac. This time I wasn't surprised by the burning feeling as it slid down my throat and found I enjoyed the taste. "So what is it about weddings that causes you to stand alone and drink?" I asked, knowing it was not my business.

Cormac swayed a little as he turned toward and I wondered how many bottles he'd had before I reached him. "It's not so much the wedding," he said. "It's the lies that they use to get them to make those kind of false commitments to each other."

"So you've had your heart broken?" I asked.

"Who hasn't though, right?" He lifted the bottle as if making a toast and then took another long swig.

I thought about his words and wondered if they were true. Did everyone experience heartbreak at some time? I experienced disappointment when my betrothed ran off rather than risk his life defending me. But it wasn't heartbreak because to be honest, I never expected anything from him. I didn't love him so he couldn't break my heart. "I wouldn't know. I've never been in love."

"Then you're lucky," Cormac said.

"I'd like to be, someday. They say being in love is the happiest you'll ever feel. Doesn't everyone want that?" I asked.

"Not if the price in the end is betrayal and feeling like you're so broken that you can never trust another living soul again." The bottle slipped from his fingers landing with a soft thud on the ground spilling its contents across the dirt.

Cormac stared at me, his eyes locked on mine and I felt flutters return to my chest. In the firelight, his features were softened and hardened at the same time, giving him both the look of an angel and something dangerous. He took a step closer to me and I could smell the alcohol on his breath. My heart seemed to beat faster the closer he got to me until we were so close we were almost touching.

"One day, someone will love you." Cormac moved a loose curl away from my face and his fingers brushed against my cheek. "You deserve to be loved. Everyone does."

He dropped his hand and ducked down to pick up the discarded bottle, took a swig, then walked away. I stood in front of the fire, my cheek still tingling from the place his fingers had touched my skin, thinking about what Cormac said.

I had never allowed myself to consider things like love. It was something that belonged in the world of faerie tales or stories for children. My father used to say that love was the one luxury afforded to the poor. People of noble birth, people who were working their way climbing up, like my family, didn't get to choose whom they wanted to marry. Marriage was a business deal, like everything else had been in my parents' home.

It was an interesting thought to consider now that I knew the people who raised me were never my parents to begin with and faerie stories turned out to be real. Did that mean it was possible to have a happily ever after? Was there such a thing as true love or finding your prince? Shivers ran down my spine as I realized I was in the company of three princes. Any of them would make a fine husband for any girl.

I hadn't known them long, but they seemed honest and loyal. Perhaps that's why Cormac had been so broken by the betrayal he suffered. He seemed the faithful type despite his rough exterior.

I looked toward the party and smiled when I caught sight of Dane with the female on his lap. He probably was an excellent lover like he claimed, but I wasn't sure fidelity was even in his vocabulary. I turned back to the fire and considered the princes.

Ethan had a heart of gold, and was by far one of the kindest and most caring males that I'd ever met in my life. Most human men were so worried about showing how tough they were that they didn't risk demonstrating their softer side. I had a feeling Ethan was exactly as he promised and was just as kind behind closed doors as he was in public.

The fire crackled in front of me, breaking me from my thoughts and I jumped a bit startled by the sound. The music had started up behind me again. Cormac was long gone, off to drink in solitude somewhere else I supposed.

I turned back to where I had come from to see the dancing once again in full swing. I couldn't help but smile at the happiness and revelry in front of me. I wondered if every event in Faerie was like this. So much joy, so much love of life, and so much happiness just being together.

My wedding would've had dancing, but it would've looked

nothing like this. Our dancing was formal and stiff and choreographed. That wasn't the case here. I moved closer to the party and noticed there was a lot more swaying and giggling and bumping into each other than there had been before dinner.

The goblets during our meal had rarely emptied before they were refilled by servants in blue tunics. Everyone was feeling the effects of the wine and were intoxicated by the music. Scanning the scene, I looked for my other escorts and found Ethan still deep in conversation at the table with the older Fae males. They were the only ones still seated and I wasn't sure what they were talking about, but it must've been very interesting.

I decided that I didn't want to interrupt him so I looked for Dane.

In the spinning and swirling of fabric and mass movement of dancing bodies, he was difficult to find. So I switched tactics and started looking for someone with red hair. That worked. I was able to find her, wrapped around Dane on the dance floor. The two were so close they were almost one body moving in time to the music. She threw her head back in laughter and Dane nuzzled his nose into her neck. They might've started the evening as strangers, but they were getting to know each other on an intimate level rather quickly.

Then, I noticed movement to the side and turned toward the disturbance. A large Fae male was pushing his way through the party goers amid grunts and shrieks of protest. I straightened, my whole body tensing as I recognized him as a predator stalking his prey. It took a moment for me to realize that he was headed right for Dane and his companion.

"Look out!" I shouted, hoping Dane would hear me through the din of the crowd.

Dane pulled his head away from his partner just in time for the newcomer's fist to make contact with Dane's face.

Chapter Seventeen

The music stopped and everyone standing near Dane and his assailant stepped back, forming a circle of onlookers who instantly started cheering on the fight. It was like watching the boys I grew up with when they got in the scuffle over something. Only this time the fighters were grown males who both looked like they knew how to fight. I wasn't sure a fight like this would end with only black eyes and bruised knuckles.

Dane rubbed his jaw and looked at his attacker with a smirk on his face. The other male glared at him with both of his hands clenched into fists. "You think you can come in here and take my mate just because you're a prince?"

"I didn't take anything. Your mate came to me."

"I'm going to enjoy killing you. You made a big mistake leaving your court. You have no authority here." The man charged, throwing another fist at Dane's face.

Dane dodged the blow with a nonchalance that made me think he might enjoy the attention.

"No harm's been done here, just some dancing," Dane said.

"Stop it, Theo," the redhead shouted.

"You think you can take whatever you want," Theo said.

"Doesn't work that way in the Autumn Court."

"If you were giving her what she needed, she'd never have come to me in the first place," Dane said.

Theo launched himself at Dane, arms wide open. He grabbed Dane around the waist and threw him to the ground. Theo was on top of Dane, straddling him.

For a few seconds it looked like he had had been pinned. But in a move so fast I barely had time to register what was happening, Dane had Theo on the ground and was standing above him, his foot on the male's chest. "I don't want to fight you. But I will if I have to."

Theo rolled out from under Dane's boot and jumped to standing himself before charging at Dane once more. Dane stepped to the side then turned back to Theo and punched him in the jaw.

The redhead was crying now, begging the males to stop fighting. Nobody paid any attention to her, but I could feel the anxiety she was experiencing.

Theo stumbled backward lifting his hand to his face, checking on the injury. Blood flowed from his lip and when he caught sight of the crimson on his fingers, his eyes narrowed. Glaring at Dane, he attacked again, this time landing a blow on Dane's upper temple.

Dane's head turned as he took the impact of the hit, but he rallied quickly. Before Theo could back away, Dane landed a knee in the male's gut. Theo doubled over, but not before he managed to put his foot out to trip Dane, knocking him to the ground.

Dane got up a little slower this time, wiping some blood off of his cheek. The sight of an actual injury set my pulse racing more than it had been. I didn't want to see him hurt and while I had a feeling he could take care of himself and he could finish this fight, I was worried it could lead to some long-term damage.

I pushed forward, trying to reach Dane, but someone held me back. "This isn't your place, female. Let the males fight."

I didn't know the male who stuck his arm in front of me and I didn't like the way he spoke to me. Irritated, I shoved his arm out of the way. "Leave me alone."

He grabbed the back of my tunic and tugged. "You'll get hurt if you go in there."

"I have to stop them," I said.

"They'll stop in a minute," he said. "It's not a wedding until someone gets in a fight."

I frowned, not liking that tradition and wondering if it was true. Pulling away from the stranger, I moved a few inches closer so I could see better, but I didn't engage.

The two males stared each other down, circling like predators. I held my breath, hoping they were almost finished with this. The longer they continued, the more chance of someone getting hurt. Or worse.

Theo made the first move, kicking Dane in the stomach, but Dane was too fast for him. He caught Theo's leg, twisting it and sending him to the ground. Dane kicked him while he was down. "Have you had enough?" Dane asked.

Theo rolled over and grabbed the back of Dane's tunic, pulling him hard until he fell to his knees. Both men were up on their feet again quickly and stared at each other.

I knew that look and I knew they weren't going to back down. This wasn't going to end any time soon. I couldn't take it anymore. This was my chance to intervene and I didn't waste it. I ran toward the fight, pushing my way through the crowd. When I reached the males, I stepped in between the two of them.

Suddenly, a fist made contact with my back and I fell, landing in Dane's arms. Stars danced in my vision and I looked back to see Theo's mouth wide open in surprise.

"Are you mad?" Dane called out. "Didn't you see her!"

"That was meant for you, not her," Theo said.

I winced and moved my arm around, making sure everything seemed to be working. I was going to be sore from this, and likely have the bruise to prove I'd been hit, but it wasn't a major injury. "I'll be fine. You two have to stop fighting."

"So you have to have your females fight your battles for you?" Theo asked.

"I'm trying to stop you two from being so stupid. Don't you see you two are just going to keep injuring each other and neither of you is going to win," I said.

"Step away, wench, before I make you," Theo said. He closed in on us and for a moment I thought he was going to hit me on purpose. Panic swelled up inside me and I knew I needed to defend myself. Without thinking I reached inside, tugging at that part of me that wanted so desperately to be free. A moment later we were surrounded by a blinding light. Somehow, I'd released the same light I had when I escaped from my father's house.

Everything was silent and in the blinding white light I felt like I had been sucked into a void. Completely deprived of my senses, I reached out in front of me trying to find something to ground me in reality. Then, my heart beat flooded my ears, thunderous and overwhelming, the only sound I could hear. I started to panic and just as I was going to cry out, a pair of strong arms wrapped around me and pulled me into a firm chest.

I breathed in the familiar scent of rosemary and honey and I felt the tension leave me. As if connected to my emotions, the light began to fade, lessening in intensity with every intake of my steady breath.

I felt someone's lips brush against my ear and a soft tingle ran down my neck and through my chest. "Deep breaths, Cassia. You're safe."

I took a deep breath in through my nose and blew it out through my mouth, focusing on slowing my racing heartbeat. I could make out shapes now, figures moving around as the light continued to fade.

I blinked a few times, adjusting to the darkness and noted that Dane and I were alone inside the circle of onlookers. Theo backed away and was holding onto the redheaded female. She seemed to have lost all interest in Dane after whatever it was that had just happened.

"What was that?" Theo asked as he pushed the redhead behind him, ready to defend her.

I looked over at Dane, desperate for him to chime in and say something. There had to be an explanation for this, but I didn't know what it was.

Dane looked just as baffled as me. Yet, he still kept his arms wrapped tightly around me protecting me from something I couldn't see. Were these other Fae going to attack me? Was that what he was worried about? The crowd parted and Cormac stumbled into the center of the group with Ethan at his heels.

"Nothing to worry about here. Just untrained magic," Cormac said.

I was surprised how clearly he was speaking considering he had a whole new bottle of wine in his hand and it didn't look like there was much left in it. How much had he had to drink tonight?

"I've never seen magic like that," Theo said, pointing an accusatory finger at me.

I pressed myself back against Dane's chest desperately seeking some protection from what I worried was going to turn into a mob. I'd seen this happen before one time in the village when my family had gone in for a festival. The crowd gathered around a woman who was accused of using magic. Terrible things were done to her that day and they all flashed through my mind as the dozens of eyes seemed to silently condemn me.

Cormac stepped in front of me with Ethan at his side. Both men crossed their arms over their chests as if threatening someone to come forward. "I've claimed protection rights over this girl. If anyone has a problem with her, they'll have to go through me," Cormac said.

"And me," Ethan said.

"And me," Dane said, pulling me closer.

My throat tightened as I swallowed down the threat of tears. My own father, and the man who had been my betrothed, along with everyone I'd known my entire life, had fled when the beast attacked me on my wedding day. Yet, these princes who'd known me for less than two days were willing to stand up and defend me. I never knew there could be such kindness and such loyalty in the world.

"This is a party," Nikolai said, pushing his way through the crowd. He stopped just inside the circle and bowed toward Cormac and Ethan. "I'm terribly sorry, your grace. We are but simple folk and some of us," he turned and glared at Theo, "forget our manners when they've had too much to drink."

"You say this girl is under your protection which means she's like family." Nikolai stepped to the side and turned to me before bowing low. "My lady, please forgive the rudeness of my guests. Would you care to join us at the head table for dessert?"

My eyes widened and I had to fight myself to keep my jaw from dropping open. I'd gone from being glared at as if I were on trial to being asked to sit at the head table.

I looked at the faces watching the scene unfold. Their expressions had softened and several of them even wore smiles on their faces. I wasn't sure what it meant that Cormac had me in his protection, but Nikolai said it made me like family. I didn't know if that was just Nikolai trying to smooth things over or if something even more significant had just occurred.

I looked to Dane and then back at Cormac and Ethan for guidance. Ethan gave a subtle nod and I took it as affirmation that I should accept the invitation. Finally feeling confident enough to step away from Dane, I gently lowered his arms from me and stepped away from his embrace.

"I would be honored." I inclined my head in a small bow.

Nikolai clapped his hands twice and practically jumped up and down. "This is a party, isn't it?" He clapped again. "Start the music and bring out the cake!"

Chapter Eighteen

Nikolai bowed to me again and offered his elbow. I gently set my hand in the crook and let him lead me away from my protectors. Part of me wanted to run back to them, to thank them. And honestly, part of me longed to be held again by Dane. If his touch was indicative of how he was as a partner, I could see why females were so interested in him. He had the most delicious balance of tenderness and masculinity that made me feel like nothing in the world could ever harm me. I wanted to hold onto that feeling because it was the first time I had truly felt safe in my life.

I glanced back over my shoulder to find the dancing was back in full swing, but none of the princes had joined in. All three of them stood just beyond the crowd watching my every move. I looked away from them, but I felt their gaze linger. It was nice to know that they were looking out for me and it was nice to feel protected.

When we reached the head table, Nikolai introduced me to his daughter and her husband. His daughter was named Mia and she rose to embrace me as if I were her sister without hesitation.

She pulled out the chair next to her and patted her hand on the seat. "Please, sit by me. You just have to tell me what it's like."

"Excuse me?" I asked.

Nikolai had wandered off, mingling with the guests, as servants carried out trays and trays of sweets. Madeleine leaned toward me conspiratorially and lowered her voice. "The princes. You arrived here with all three of them. Nobody's even seen Prince Cormac with a female in a hundred years. What did you do to get all three of them to follow you around? And to get him to take you under his protection? You must be someone very important or he's deeply in love with you. Plus, I've heard rumors about Prince Dane, even here in the Autumn Court, he's got a reputation."

My chest felt tight as I stared at the smiling bride. "It was sort of fate, I suppose." I wasn't sure what to say. *Do I explain that the Sodalis are after me?* That wasn't something that someone would want to hear on their wedding day. And the more I thought about it, the less I liked being there. Creatures really were hunting me, was I going to lead them here into all these people? An attack on a crowded place like this could cost so many people their lives. My heart raced and I suddenly felt hot.

"You know, it isn't often that the right of protection is evoked. Does that mean he's taking you to the Queen's Trial? Or are you his mistress or more?"

There were too many questions and I didn't know what any of them meant. I wanted to ask her what this *right of protection* was, but I was afraid if I didn't know, it would lead to too many questions about me and where I came from. She stared at me with a hopeful expression and I knew I wasn't going to get away with silence. "We're working on something together. I'm not romantically involved with any of them."

"Oh," she said, looking disappointed. "Academy business, I suppose?"

I smiled and made a noncommittal noise, hoping it would

appease her. I had no idea what the Academy was, but if it kept her from asking any more questions, I'd play along.

Thankfully, before she could ask or say anything else, Nikolai clapped his hands again and asked for the music to stop. "As tradition dictates, those who have not yet found their mate will choose the first piece of cake."

"Go on," Mia urged me giving me a little push. "If you don't go, everyone is going to think you're involved with the princes."

That was enough for me. Besides, the cake was beautiful and probably tasted amazing.

Hesitantly, I stood and walked toward the two-tiered cake that was the centerpiece of the sweet and dessert spread. Blue dressed servants were slicing up the top layer of cake and plating it. The Fae lingering around the table waited patiently for their slice. I glanced back at the long tables where we'd eaten dinner and saw that about half of the guests were still seated. Apparently, it was a pretty even split of married and unmarried Fae.

Ethan walked over to where I was standing and stopped so close to me that his arm pressed against mine. He leaned down and whispered, "Traditionally, the top layer is made with wild raspberries. The legend is, that eating raspberries at a wedding will help you to meet your mate sooner."

A maid in a blue dress handed me a plate and I looked down to see the red ribbons of fruit spreading through the white cake. The maid handed Ethan a plate and he took it from her then lifted it toward me in a toast before taking a bite. "I'm not sure that it works, but it sure is delicious."

I took a bite of my own cake and had to stop myself from letting my eyes roll into the back of my head. It was the most heavenly thing I had ever tasted. The cake melted on my tongue leaving a burst of sweet and tart from the raspberry all at the same time. I had never tasted cake like this at home.

"Next, we invite those who are mated, but have yet to produce their offspring," Nikolai said.

Brow furrowed, I looked up at Ethan hoping for another explanation.

"The next layer is lavender. To help with fertility," he said.

Another group, including the bride and groom, came forward and took the lavender slices of cake. One woman giggled as she fed a bite to her husband. Finally, Nikolai invited the last group of people to come for dessert. "For those of you who have your children and your mates please come and enjoy the desserts."

The last few remaining guests stood and gathered around the dessert table, though they ate none of the cake. It seemed the cake was reserved for those who still needed something. The rest of the dessert was for those who had gained the things the Fae seemed to value. In this way, the Faerie realm wasn't much different from the human realm. They still seemed interested in making sure everyone was married off and produced heirs. Suddenly, the cake didn't taste so good. I set my fork down and looked around for a place to abandon the plate. Before I could find something, one of the maids swept up to me and held out her hands. "Are you finished, lady?"

"Thank you," I said as I passed the plate.

"Wait," Ethan said, grabbing the plate from the maid's hand. "If she's not going to eat it, I will. I can use all the help I can get."

He winked and the maid giggled, covering her mouth with her hand before ducking away from us.

"I'm sure it's not difficult for a prince to find a mate," I said. "You must have females waiting in line to marry you."

"It doesn't work the same way here as it does in the human realm," he said. "Marriage isn't about alliance and it's not exactly about love. Mating is deeper than that. It's a union of souls and when you find the one who completes your soul, you bond with them and you never let them go. It's a pure and complete connection, it takes over. The only thing you can think about is your mate and their well-being. You begin to anticipate their needs and you begin to know how they feel even when you're apart."

"It didn't seem that way with Theo and his mate," I said.

Ethan laughed. "That wasn't about love or mating, that was about sex."

My eyes widened.

"Some Fae take lovers even if they have a mate." Ethan took another bite of cake.

"It's so different than the human realm," I said. "What if you never come across the one you're supposed to mate with?" The idea of arranged marriages was frightening enough, but the idea of possibly waiting your whole life to find the one you were meant to be with was even more frightening.

"It's not exactly known how it works. They say it's possible to have more than one mate out there for you just in case you don't find one of them right away. Our queen has three mates, so I guess anything is possible," he said.

"But how do you find the right one?" I asked.

"I suspect it might be similar to how some humans do. It's not usually an instant bond. Attraction, yes, but then you have to spend some time to get to know them to see if it's real," he said.

"What if you left before you took that time?" I asked.

"If you met your mate and left, you'd find yourself drawn back to the place you left them," Ethan said. "It could be why Cormac continues to visit Angela on occasion. She broke his heart, but he still can't shake her."

I opened my mouth to ask about Angela and Cormac, but Ethan held up a hand. "If you're going to ask, don't. It's not my story to tell."

I closed my mouth and thought about everything Ethan had said. Fae relationships seemed complicated. How were you ever to find the one you were meant to be with? What if you were a peasant and you never left the village you were born in? "It could take a lifetime to find your mate."

"For some people, it might take centuries, but we're immortal," he said.

That stopped me dead in my tracks. I hadn't stopped to think about the fact that the Fae didn't age like humans. What did that mean for me? It was difficult to comprehend that I wasn't going to continue to grow old the way the humans that I knew had.

So many questions occurred to me at that very moment. I had nothing. No skills, no money, no lands and no home. But there was hope now of finding those things in the best way possible.

In my old life, the best I could hope for was to grow fond of my husband after I married him. Maybe, after everything I'd been through, I could still find someone who completed me. Who wouldn't want that? If I found that, I would have the belonging I so longed for and we could make a home together.

Perhaps that was my best plan when this was all over. I didn't have anything else to hope for. Maybe I could find that companionship I craved. I wondered if that was even possible for me. I wondered if the fact that I was a changeling and that I'd grown up in the human world would somehow ruin me. Was there still someone out there for me?

As if he knew what I was thinking, Ethan reached down and grabbed my hand in his, giving it a squeeze. "All Fae find their mates eventually. For some, it takes more time. But we always find them."

I squeezed his hand back and smiled. There was too much going on in my head for me to string together a coherent thought.

In front of us, guests were finishing up their desserts and the music started up again. "How long does the party last?"

"The longest wedding I ever went to was three days," Ethan said. "I've heard of celebrations that last weeks."

"Don't you have things to do?" I asked. I wasn't exactly in a rush to go on a monster hunt and I certainly wasn't in a rush to leave these princes behind. They'd become so important to me in such a short time that it was difficult to imagine my life without them.

"Most of the small-town weddings wrap up by dawn," he said. "Come dance."

I let Ethan lead me to the dance floor where he taught me another Faerie dance that left me breathless. And I enjoyed every second. It felt so good not to be worrying about anything. But all good things came to an end. Just as Ethan predicted, as the first light of the sun broke the horizon, the band played the last song.

"May I?" Cormac asked.

I turned, startled by his presence. Cormac had made it very clear how he felt about weddings.

Ethan bowed and let go of my hand backing away from the dancers. Cormac stood in front of me, arm outstretched. I set my hand inside his waiting palm and noticed how fragile and small my hand looked inside of his. I might be Fae, but the males were much larger than me.

Cormac instantly used size to his advantage and lifted me off the ground spinning me in a circle before setting me back down. The move caught me by surprise and I found that I was smiling so wide that my face started to hurt. Cormac smiled back and without a word, continued the dance. Cormac was much more graceful than I expected and he guided me through the steps of the unfamiliar dance.

When the song ended, my heart sank. I wasn't ready for it to be over and I wasn't ready to let go of Cormac's hands. We stood there for a moment, my hands locked in his, both of us breathing heavily from exertion as the floor cleared around us.

"Your grace," Nikolai called.

Cormac dropped my hands abruptly and turned to face our host.

"If you allow me, I'll show you the way to my estate."

The interruption left me wondering what may have come to pass between us had we been given just a few more minutes. While I wanted to be upset about Nikolai's timing, I couldn't help but smile as I followed him and the princes.

Chapter Nineteen

The term estate wasn't quite accurate to describe Nikolai's house. At least not by human realm standards. It was a comfortable home with four bedrooms, a dining space, living room with a modest fireplace, and a good sized kitchen. He even had two bathrooms so guests didn't need to share with their host.

Compared to Cormac's home, there was nothing impressive about Nikolai's. Though, I'd seen families crammed into one room shacks the size of a horse stable who would gladly live in a place like this. To some, this would be luxurious. Nikolai was proud of his home, taking us from room to room and showing all of the things he had updated and improved. He pointed out the polished wood floors throughout the home, the tapestries on the walls, and the sparkling stone he'd used to trim his fireplace.

All of the furniture in the home was well loved and well worn. In a way, it was refreshing to see things that actually got use. Aside from my bedroom growing up, my family had seemed almost afraid to use the furniture in most of our living areas. They were obsessed with keeping it in pristine quality so we could show off the wealth we didn't have when people came to visit.

Finally, we arrived at the guest bedrooms. I could see the sun shining through the open windows of the first room and realized it had been a full day and night since I'd last slept. Focusing on the joy of getting some rest, I lost track of what Nikolai and Cormac were discussing and made myself rejoin the conversation.

"And if you prefer," Nikolai said. "You're welcome to use my room as well."

"That won't be necessary, these accommodations are more than adequate," Cormac said.

"Your house is lovely," I added when I noticed Nikolai's slightly crestfallen face at Cormac's comment. "Your family is very lucky to live here."

Nikolai inclined his head. "Thank you, lady. You are too kind."

His eyes swept over the four of us and then he pointed to the bathroom down the hall. "There are fresh towels and everything you should need in there."

"Thank you for your hospitality, Nikolai," Cormac said.

"If there's anything you need at all don't hesitate to knock on my door," Nikolai said.

As he walked away, I wondered where the blue dressed servants were. The party had lots of servants present to help with all the details whereas none of them appeared in Nikolai's home. I wondered if that meant he didn't have any of his own or if he'd given them the time off. Either option actually made me like him better.

"Cassia, which room would you prefer?" Ethan asked. "The rest of us can share the other."

"You want her to sleep alone with the monsters after her?" Dane asked. "I for one, would feel better if I were in there with her."

"I'm sure you would, Dane," said Ethan.

"She'll be fine," Cormac said. "There were so many people tonight filling the air with their scent that the beasts won't be able to track her for hours."

"I'll be fine." I turned to Dane. "Thank you for your concern."

I turned and selected the door nearest me, opening it just wide enough for me to slide through before closing it behind me. I didn't want to hear any other objections and I didn't want anything between me and some rest.

Despite my hesitation about joining in the festivities for someone else's wedding, it had been a thrilling and exciting evening. I couldn't remember the last time I truly had fun. Right now, I was tired and could use some time to clear my head.

I unlaced the trousers I was wearing and let them drop to the floor in a puddle before stepping out of them. Then, I pulled the tunic up over my head and tossed it aside. As I walked toward the large comfortable looking bed I unpinned my hair until it hung loose down my back.

I didn't have any night clothes to wear so I slipped in between the sheets in my sheer undergarments and settled into the soft pillows. I wondered if I should be worried about the Sodalis or even about our host. In the human realm, I never would have felt safe sleeping in a stranger's house. But there was something comforting about knowing that the three princes were in the room across the hall.

Somehow, I knew Cormac's words were correct. I had felt safe while I was at that wedding and I wasn't sure why. But even for someone who didn't understand hunting, his theory made sense. The sheer amount of guests at the party dancing and moving and sweating had to send a very mixed scent to a predator in the area. Pinpointing specific scents would be difficult.

I snuggled down under the fluffy quilt, letting my eyelids grow heavy. Tomorrow, I knew we would begin the long process of tracking and hunting the monsters. But tonight, I got to sleep in a warm bed and I didn't want to waste a second of it because I knew once we were on the road, finding a good place to sleep might be more difficult.

SOMETHING WOKE ME, sending an uncomfortable prickle down my spine. I kept my eyes closed and listened for a second, almost afraid to open them. My first fear was that the monsters had found me and that when I opened my eyes I'd be staring at the fanged mouth of one of those horrid creatures.

I took a deep breath and realized the air smelled fresh like citrus and cedar. The monsters smelled like death.

Feeling a little braver, I opened one eye then the other and let out a sigh of relief as I realized the presence I was sensing in my room wasn't a monster. At least I hoped he wasn't a monster. I supposed that despite the bond and the safety I felt around the princes, I didn't really know any of them yet. And Cormac with his brooding temperaments and drinking and tough guy exterior, could be hiding something for all I knew.

I scooted back against the pillows pushing myself up to sitting as I calmly waited for Cormac to explain why he was on the end of my bed lounging in a position that gave me the sense he'd been there a while.

"You were talking in your sleep," he said.

"I don't talk in my sleep," I said.

"You were. I've been sitting here for hours," he said.

"Hours?" I asked. Then I realized I was wearing next to nothing and I grabbed the covers and pulled them up over my chest. "Why?"

"As I said, you were talking in your sleep."

"That's generally not a reason to come in and stare at someone while they're sleeping," I said. "It's creepy, and weird."

Cormac smirked. "Well, you did say my name a few times."

"You're making that up."

He shoved himself up from the bed and stood, raising his arms above his head to stretch. He made a good show of twisting and turning, pulling his tunic tight around him, showing off all of his sculpted form. "If you say so." He dropped his arms to his side and leisurely walked toward the bedroom door. He paused with his hand on the doorknob. "Breakfast is ready. You might want to put some clothes on or I won't be responsible for what Dane does to you."

"Wait," I called after Cormac. He stopped with the door open behind him and then turned to look at me.

"What did you mean when you said I'm under your protection?" I asked.

Cormac closed the door and took a few steps forward, pausing before he reached me. "Everything we do and say here has meaning. I'm sure you've heard that the Fae can't tell a lie. That's not entirely true, but it's close. We don't lie because we don't need to lie. We know that words have power. When I said that you were under my protection, that doesn't mean right now or until I get bored. It means that I promise to look out for you no matter what."

"Why? You don't even know me."

"I'm not sure," he said. "And that's not like me. I always think before I speak. I've never been one to let my emotions get the better of me. But for some reason, you seem to bring that out of me."

"I can't tell if that's a good thing or a bad thing," I said.

"Neither can I." He turned and he left, closing the door behind him.

I was sure Cormac was getting tired of my questions; they probably all were. I really wanted to ask them about the magic that I unleashed, but the way that everyone had reacted made me think it might be a better idea to leave it alone. It wasn't the first time I had done it. It seemed to come out when I was afraid and feeling cornered. I wondered why I hadn't let it out when I was attacked by the beasts. I certainly felt cornered and afraid in those situations. But something about angry men coming after me was even more terrifying than a monster.

I slid off the bed and scowled at the pants I had left in a wrinkled pile on the floor. I probably should've hung them over a chair. I stepped into the pants and pulled them up, grateful that Cormac's maids had found me something suitable to wear. I wondered why he had them at his house. The trousers were far too small for any of the males to wear. Did he have a sister that I didn't know about? Or perhaps they belonged to a love interest who had spent time at his home. I knew that was an answer to a question I wasn't going to get out of Cormac.

I used my fingers to brush out my hair as I walked down the stairs toward the living spaces. Cormac, Ethan, and Dane were seated around a table with Nikolai.

All four males rose to greet me when they saw me and inclined their heads toward me followed by a chorus of, "Good morning."

I managed a weak curtsy. "Good morning."

Dane was the first on his feet in front of an empty chair and pulled it out for me. I took the seat and he shoved me and a little harder than he probably should've. "Thank you."

As soon as he resumed his seat, the other men sat and they all stared at me.

"Did you sleep well?" I asked the room in general, hoping to break the silence.

"Excellent, thank you," Nikolai said, not giving the others a chance to speak. "And you, my lady?"

"It was like sleeping on a cloud. Your home is a wonderful place," I said.

Bowls of food were passed to me and I quickly filled a plate as the others watched me in silence. I wondered what kind of conversation I'd interrupted. "Did we sleep through most of the day?" I asked.

"We've got about four hours of sunlight," Cormac said. "We'll have enough light to ride for a while before we stop."

I took a bite of a yellow fruit and had another piece on my fork before I even swallowed. It was juicy and much sweeter than the fruit I'd eaten at my old home. "What is this called?" I asked, lifting up the fruit.

"It's a peach," Nikolai said. "We grow them in our orchards. I'll send some with you when you leave."

"It's delicious," I said, eating my next bite.

"It's my favorite," Nikolai said. "What's your favorite food, your grace?"

I turned to look at Cormac. He looked displeased to be asked such a trivial question. "Anything with cinnamon."

"Not me, give me a big piece of meat," Dane said.

The males continued to talk about food while I ate my breakfast, smiling and nodding along to their conversation. Nikolai was gifted at small talk. I could see why he was the mayor of the small town. He made you feel at ease, comfortable. By the time he steered into childhood memories of skinned knees and climbing trees, everyone had finished their breakfast.

"Nikolai, thank you for your hospitality. When we return, I would very much like to have you and your family over for dinner at my estate," Cormac said.

Nikolai's eyes widened and the color momentarily drained from his face. He looked like someone had just handed him the very thing he always dreamed of. I'd seen that look before, on my father's face every time something happened to give him a step closer to climbing the social ladder. I hadn't initially pegged Nikolai for a social climber, but I supposed they had to exist here just the same as they did in the human realm.

Nikolai clapped his hands and nodded eagerly. "Thank you, your grace. That would be an honor for me and my family."

Cormac stood, and Ethan and Dane followed. Ethan walked around the table to my chair and helped me from my seat. The formality was rather interesting considering the casual way they'd all interacted with me on our first few days together. I wondered if it was something they were interested in doing and had just forgotten their manners, or if this was all a show for Nikolai. I supposed I would find out as soon as we were on the road together.

I turned to Nikolai and curtsied once again, feeling like I probably should say something in the form of a goodbye. "Thank you for your hospitality, kind sir."

Nikolai's eyes shone bright and excited. Hosting the princes had probably been the highlight of his night. When he told the story of his daughter's wedding, I had a feeling the fact that three princes turned up would be the most often retold part of the tale.

Chapter Twenty

It turned out, that the stolen hours spent riding my horse starting at a young age were worth their weight in gold. I was an experienced rider, so I could keep up with the princes, but I knew had it been my sister, Rose, in this position, she would've given up after the first hour in the saddle.

We continued down the road, passing sparsely dotted villages and the occasional farmland. I wondered if this was how everything looked here, miles between your nearest neighbor and town so small they made the one I grew up in look like a city.

I'd never actually been to a city, but I'd heard stories of cobblestone streets, buildings taller than three or four stories, and the possibility to buy anything you could dream of. I also heard they were crowded, smelly, and dangerous. Perhaps it was good we hadn't come across any cities, though my curiosity hummed in the background.

There was a constant internal vibration begging me to see as much as I could and experience as much as I could. I wanted to see everything, taste everything, and smell everything. It was as if I had just been born and everything was fresh and new and unfamiliar. It should have scared me, but I found it just made me more curious and more excited, driving the anticipation of what would be beyond the next hilltop as we rode along.

After riding in single file in silence for hours, loneliness tightened in my chest. I wondered if this was the way they always rode or if the addition of me in their party had silenced the princes. They seemed to know each other so well, yet they each came from a different court.

Cormac was upfront, with me behind him followed by Dane and Ethan. The road was wide enough and we hadn't seen any other travelers for a while so I pulled on the reins and picked up pace enough so that I could ride alongside Cormac.

He looked over at me as I settled into pace next to him. "Everything all right?"

"It's a long ride to complete in silence," I said. "Is this how you always travel?"

"When you're tracking animals, it's usually best to remain quiet so you don't let them know you're on to them," he said.

"Those monsters didn't seem to have any problem coming out with lots of noise around. Maybe they like noise," I said with a shrug.

Cormac turned again and lifted an eyebrow as he studied me for a moment. "That's an interesting observation. It's possible the creatures are attracted to noise, but they didn't attack the night of the wedding."

I slumped a bit in my saddle, the moment of smugness leaching out of me. "That's true."

"Where are we going anyway?" I asked.

"We got word that a few of the Sodalis made a home in the woods outside of Twin Falls. It seemed as good a place as any to begin," Cormac said.

"What is Twin Falls?" I asked.

"It's both a town and a place in the woods. A pair of twin waterfalls drew settlers to the area and they named their town after them."

"How much farther?" I asked, trying not to come across as tired and ready to get off the horse. I was still holding up okay for now, but I knew it wouldn't be long before I would tire. Plus, the sun was dangerously low to setting and I wasn't thrilled with the idea of being out overnight.

"You see that hill?" Cormac asked.

I nodded even though he couldn't see me.

"Just beyond the hill there's a farmhouse owned by a friend of mine. We'll stay there for the night and ride into Twin Falls first thing in the morning. We don't want to be trying to hunt the creatures at night."

Normally, when it came to hunting, my stomach would turn at the thought. But these beasts were vicious and evil creatures. I wasn't even sure they had a thought beyond maiming. Then I realized, so far in all my encounters, they'd been after only me. "Are these monsters always like this? Do they always attack or do they normally behave differently?"

"They are different than other animals, if that's what you're asking," Cormac said. "Most of the creatures we hunt ignore us unless we cause a threat. The creatures from the Under are not like that."

"What's the Under like? What makes the animals there so different?" I asked.

"It's a vicious world full of more dark creatures than you could ever imagine and they all have one goal. They destroy. They kill and then they reclaim any land they can. We think that if we let them out on their own, they would destroy our world until it was as broken and desolate as their own."

I shuddered and my skin felt like it was crawling. I couldn't imagine a world full of monsters like the Sodalis and I couldn't even picture a monster that was worse. "What happens after you kill them all?"

"They'll keep coming unless we seal the tear," he said. "It's usually nearby a nest. So far, we've found four nests and no tear.

I'm hoping we'll find it here."

"Do you usually have that many nests?" I asked.

"No."

"Why do you think it changed?" I could see a touch of fear on Cormac's expression. It was gone in an instant, but it was there. It was an expression I hoped I never saw again.

"This time, there's more of them than we've ever seen before. And this time, there's you. We've never seen them go after a specific Fae before, at least not that we could tell. I don't know if that means there's something about you or if that means there's something changing about the Under," Cormac said.

My heart hammered against my ribs as I considered Cormac's words. I didn't feel like there was anything about me that might cause such a disturbance, but then again, I didn't even know I was Fae until two days ago. I was quiet as I rode alongside Cormac, letting my thoughts swim in my mind. I didn't know anything about myself anymore. I had no past and no future. It was like living in limbo and the confidence and excitement I'd felt at the beginning of the ride faded.

Would I have to keep feeling this disconnected for the rest of my existence or would I find answers some day? I wished there was a way to figure out why I'd been placed in the human world and where I came from. But whoever hid me there clearly didn't want me out. Though, I supposed I wasn't limited to human time constraints anymore. Would it take me a century to find out where I came from? Longer? Would I feel this out of place still after a few years of living in this realm?

"Cassia?"

Cormac's voice broke my reverie. "Yes?"

He glanced at me and one corner of his lips pulled up into a smirk. "Think you can keep up?"

He didn't give me time to answer before he took off on his horse leaving a cloud of dust behind him.

I laughed and tightened my grip on the reins. "Let's go get him, Starlight."

Leaning in close, I picked up speed, following the dust cloud. My mind cleared as the wind rushed past me. My hair whipped around me, but I ignored it, concentrating on my ride. Starlight seemed to work with me, understanding what I wanted without any commands. Even though she'd been riding with me for such a short time, we learned to trust one another.

I could see Cormac now and I pushed Starlight harder. We were so close. Then, suddenly, she slowed and reared, throwing me from the saddle. I landed hard on the ground, knocking the wind from my lungs.

Grateful that I didn't smack my head on the hard dirt, I rolled away quickly so I wouldn't get trampled by a frightened horse. In the confusion, Starlight had kicked up so much dust, I couldn't see where she was. Somewhere nearby, she whinnied.

"Starlight, where are you, girl?" I called, extending my arms in front of me. "It's alright, girl."

I tried to keep my voice calm and soothing. Something startled her and I didn't want to add to her anxiety.

Instead of hearing the gentle neigh of my mare, a screeching cry sounded. I tensed and turned toward the noise slowly. In the dissipating dust I could now make out the shape of three of the bat creatures. They'd found me.

Chapter Twenty-One

F ear shot through me, making me feel like my insides were on fire and pulsing with a strange vibration. The beast's back was to me and now that the dust settled, I saw it had Cormac pinned to the ground.

Inside, that familiar feeling clawed at me as if trying to tear my skin open. Whatever it was inside me, it seemed to show up in these moments and when I fought against it, bad things happened. When I let my guard down, and let the thing out, it triggered something. Some kind of magic I didn't understand or know how to control.

Cormac was in danger and I had to save him. It was time to give in to the monster inside. I dropped my guard as I rushed toward him, willing whatever it was to come out. *Help him*, I thought. *Help him.*

As I approached the creature, it turned toward me. Nostrils flaring, it bared its teeth, letting out a low growl.

"Run, Cassia," Cormac shouted.

"Leave him alone," I said through gritted teeth. The fear inside bubbled over until it resembled anger. I was furious that these creatures were hunting me, I was overwhelmed at finding out I wasn't human, I was terrified of spending the rest of an eternal life alone.

Cormac, and the other Fae princes had been the only shining beacon of hope in the most confusing time of my life. I couldn't let anything bad happen to him. Especially knowing that I was the cause of the monster finding us.

I grabbed hold of a threat from the clawing, writhing beast inside me, and I pulled it taught. A moment later, the now familiar blinding white light radiated out from me and I flinched as I squinted against the intensity of it.

I needed to find Cormac. I needed to get him away to safety or needed to end the beast's life. Or both. One way or another, I was getting out of there with Cormac alive.

I need to see, I thought. *I need to see.* Squinting into the light, I forced myself to keep my eyes open to search for my fallen friend. The light was still glowing too bright, but I found I was able to fight against it and looked around without the pain I'd had in the past. Pushing ahead, I looked around for my fallen prince.

Cormac was on the ground ahead of me, the beast still over him. Wishing I had a weapon, I squared my shoulders and ran forward. If nothing else, maybe I could muster enough strength to drag Cormac away while the beast was distracted.

As I drew nearer, I realized the claws of the creature were digging into Cormac's leg, pinning him to the ground. If I moved Cormac without dispatching the beast first, I would damage his leg even more.

Something glinted in the light, catching my eye. I turned to see Cormac's sword lying on the ground next to him, just out of his reach. He'd been so close to finishing the creature. If he just had that in his hand, I knew he could stop this whole thing. I ran for it, pausing next to Cormac. I could hear his ragged breathing and I took a step closer to him, kneeling down with his sword in my hand. He was too weak to fight. I'd have to finish the creature myself.

"I'm going to get you out of here."

"No, Cassia, run," Cormac said, his words strained.

Ignoring him, I picked up the sword with two hands half dragging it, half carrying it toward the creature.

The beast's nostrils flared again and it snapped its jaws in my direction. Clearly, he could smell me, but couldn't see me. And that gave me an advantage.

Without thinking about what I was about to do, I angled the sword up and shoved it into the monster's throat. Warm blood spurted out covering me in foul smelling warm, wet goo. I let go of the sword and turned away from the creature and threw up on the ground. Behind me, the beast made a sickening gurgling sound. Still retching, I glanced behind me just in time to see the monster stagger and fall in a heap on its side.

I turned away again, and wiped my mouth with the back of my hand. It was covered in blood, making my stomach flip again. I closed my eyes for a moment and took a deep breath. After I collected myself, I turned back and saw the creature lying on its side, its claws still in Cormac's injured leg. I wasn't done yet.

Hands shaking and holding back bile in my throat, I approached Cormac just as the white light was fading.

I knelt down next to his leg and Cormac propped himself up on his elbows. His face was pale. "You are full of surprises."

"This is going to hurt," I said.

"Just do it," he said, tensing his jaw.

As gently as I could, I pried the claws of the dead beast out of Cormac's thigh.

Cormac grunted and I watched his hands ball into fists; his forearms and biceps flexing in tight knots of muscle against the pain.

Just as I removed the final claw, Ethan and Dane crouched down beside me.

"What happened?" Ethan asked, his hand already hovering above Cormac's injury.

"Why did you to ride off like that?" asked Dane. "You're the one who set the bloody stay together rule."

"I suppose that's why I set the rules," Cormac said in a hiss. "When I break them, bad things happen."

While Ethan worked his magic on Cormac's leg, I knelt near his head. I brushed his dark hair off his forehead away from his eyes then leaned in closer to him, keeping my eyes locked on his.

Cormac winced.

"Stay still and it'll go faster," Ethan said.

I glanced over at Ethan and watched in amazement as his skin regrew in front of my eyes. Cormac made a hissing sound and I turned back to him.

"I'm sorry," I said. Guilt surged through me because I knew Cormac wouldn't have ridden off recklessly like that if not for me. He was trying to cheer me up and keep my mind preoccupied. If it weren't for me, he wouldn't have been as distracted as he was and he would've seen the creature.

"I'll be fine. Don't worry about me," Cormac said. "How are you feeling?"

"I'm not the one who was attacked this time," I said.

"That should get you through for now," Ethan said. "I want to do another round when we stop for the night. Cormac grunted as he pushed himself up to standing. He offered his hands to me and pulled me up.

I wanted to ask him how he was feeling and tell him that he shouldn't be concerned about me while he was trying to recover, I had a feeling he wouldn't appreciate me babying him.

Cormac placed two fingers at his lips and whistled. Both his horse and mine came running to join us. As Cormac walked toward his horse, I noticed he was limping, favoring his injured leg.

Ethan offered his interlaced fingers for me to climb on Starlight's saddle. Wordlessly, I accepted the support and hopped back up on my horse. Apparently, the princes were interested in no discussion about what just happened.

Ethan rode ahead, taking the point position while I rode alongside Cormac.

"Are you all right to be riding?" I asked.

Cormac looked at me and shook his head. "You should be more worried about yourself than me."

"I'm not the one who had monster claws in my leg," I said.

"Yes, but you should have run like I told you to," Cormac said.

"You can't be angry at me. I saved your life," I said.

"I would've taken care of it on my own. I don't want anything bad happening to you."

"Is this because of that protection thing?" I asked. "Or because you don't like that a girl saved you?"

Cormac chuckled. "Spoken like a human."

"You told me yourself I'm not human, but you won't explain anything to me so that I can understand what it means to be Fae," I said.

"You're right," he said. "And it has nothing to do with the fact that you're female or even that I placed you under my protection. Maybe I just don't like the idea of you getting hurt."

I was surprised by his response and I opened my mouth, intent on saying something clever, and closed it again, speechless.

Cormac clicked his tongue and rode ahead of me, joining Ethan. I stayed behind the two of them in stunned silence for several minutes. The road was wide enough that I could join them, but I wasn't sure what I'd say. In the short time I'd spent with all of these males, I'd grown rather fond of each of them. Before I could talk myself into riding up to join the other two, Dane sped up until he was matching my pace.

"It was really brave, what you did back there. It shows you're a true Fae. In our realm, everyone learns to fight. Male and female," Dane said.

"Except me. I got lucky. Don't tell Cormac. But I was never

taught to fight. I was just as likely to drop the sword on the ground as I was to get it through the creature's throat," I said.

"That might be true, but this isn't the first monster you killed," Dane said. "We might've wounded the beast that attacked you at your wedding, but you delivered the final blow. Never forget that," he said.

I had forgotten. In all the chaos and excitement, I still saw myself as someone who was incapable of fighting back. Yet, in times of crisis, I reacted on instinct. Then there was the magic, that part of me that I was finally starting to let out. "Dane, what is the light that I create? That's magic, right?"

"Yes, it's magic. Though, I've never seen anything exactly like it. I have a theory that it happens as a defensive reaction. It's not a fully formed use of magic, but I think it's your magic trying to break through in its untrained, raw form. I saw something similar, once, when I was training some new fighters at the Academy."

"New fighters at where?" I asked.

"Don't look so shocked," he said. "I'm not all tough guy and brawn, I have a brain too."

"That's not what I meant," I said. "I just didn't picture you as a teacher."

"We all have our secrets, Cassia," Dane said. "I hope to one day learn some of yours."

I swallowed the lump in my throat and turned away from Dane as my imagination kicked in and for a moment, I saw a flash of Dane and me tangled in the sheets. A bead of sweat slid down my back and I hoped nobody could see inside my head. Being around these three males was starting to make me feel like an animal in heat. I'd never felt any desires like this with any of my childhood friends and I certainly never felt anything like this toward Aaron in our brief encounters. There was just something about them that made me feel so alive in ways I never knew I could feel.

Ethan and Cormac turned off of the main road onto a path

that looked like it had been forged by the wheels of a cart through tall, yellow grass. We weren't within view of the farmhouse we were heading to, but I knew we had to be close since we were leaving the road behind us. I blew out a relieved breath. The sooner I could get behind a closed door and get some space from the princes, the better. I wasn't sure I could be trusted with them much longer without saying something I shouldn't.

Chapter Twenty-Two

F inally, we reached the farmhouse. My legs were stiff as I dismounted with Dane's help. After taking a moment to brush the red-brown dust from my clothes, I twisted my hair into a knot at the back of my head to get it out of my way. Everything hurt. My thighs burned and my arms were sore from the day of riding.

Cormac limped up to the house and opened the door. Nobody came out to greet us.

"Didn't you say your friend lived here?" I asked.

"He does, but he's at the market in the Summer Court this time of year. We'll clean up after ourselves, if that's what you're worried about," Cormac said.

"I'm not worried about that," I said. "It just seems rude to enter someone's house when they aren't home."

"Not big on hospitality in the mortal realm, are they?" Dane asked. "We help our neighbors here."

I frowned. In theory, we had to offer hospitality to our neighbors in the mortal realm, but I'd never traveled enough to test it out. "I'm not sure. I never traveled much before coming here."

"Really?" Ethan asked. "You're such a natural on the horse I thought for sure you'd had experience with days of riding."

"I rode as often as I could," I said. "But never for travel. Only for leisure."

Ethan lifted an eyebrow. "With your fast healing ability, I thought you might be Spring Court, but it seems I may be mistaken. Perhaps you're more at home in the Autumn Court."

I shrugged. "Maybe I have talents from different courts."

"That's very unusual, but I suppose we won't know until we see some more magic from you," Ethan said.

I liked the idea of learning how to use magic. Especially if there was something that could protect me better from the Sodalis than the white light I was able to conjure. "Maybe someone can teach me?" I glanced over at Dane and smiled sweetly.

"Don't look at me. I taught combat. Ethan or Cormac would be much better suited to helping a new Fae with magic," Dane said.

I followed the males into the farmhouse. It was dark inside as all the windows were covered with shutters. Cormac lit an oil lamp which cast a warm glow over the tiny space. Despite the cloths covering all the furniture, I thought I could make out a sitting area arranged in front of a wood burning stove and a dining table with four chairs. The kitchen was out in the open, right behind the table. A staircase leading up completed the space. It was even smaller than Nikolai's house.

Ethan busied himself in front of the wood stove while Cormac and Dane removed the sheets from the furniture. I looked around, wondering what I could help with.

Someone grunted and I turned toward the sound just in time to see Ethan grabbing at his shoulder. In the flickering firelight from the newly built fire, I noticed there was a pool of blood on his tunic. How had I not noticed that before?

I walked over to him and touched his upper arm gently. "What happened?"

He looked at my hand, then his eyes traveled to the injury on his shoulder. "It's nothing."

I pursed my lips, not believing him, and tugged at the fabric. Claw marks slashed down his shoulder. They were still open wounds, but they weren't bleeding anymore. He must have been scratched during the fight. I was so focused on Cormac I didn't pay attention to where Ethan and Dane were. My stomach tightened. I should have taken better care of them. I felt like I let them down. "Why isn't it healing?"

"It's not as bad as it looks," he said, carefully removing my hand from his arm.

"But you usually heal so quickly." My brow furrowed in worry. Was something different? If he couldn't heal this, what did that mean?

"It'll heal after I get some rest. I used most of my magic to help Cormac heal. Our magic isn't unlimited. It takes a lot of energy to heal. That's why you are so tired afterward. But like I said, it's not so bad. You won't even notice it by morning." He smiled.

"You three are close, aren't you?" I asked.

"We grew up together," he said.

"But you're from different courts and you're all royalty. How is that possible?" I asked.

"You keep getting us confused with the way things work in the human world," Ethan said. "Here, most noble children are trained at the Royal Academy. The three of us were often trained together since we are all the heirs to our respective courts."

"You don't fight over land?" I asked.

He shook his head. "Why would we? Besides, if we did, the queen would get involved. And none of us want that. As long as we can govern ourselves without incident, the queen lets us do what we want."

"It sounds so uncomplicated," I said.

He laughed. "There are lots of complications. But they have a way of getting worked out."

"Who's hungry?" Dane called.

"I'm hungry, what did you bring?" Ethan called.

I followed him to the table where Dane and Cormac were already sitting. A meal of cheese, fruit, bread, and nuts sat in the middle of the table.

"Compliments of Nikolai. He insisted we bring something with us," Dane said, taking a bite of bread.

I grabbed an apple and took a bite of the sweet and tart fruit. Juice dribbled down my chin and I wiped it off with the back of my hand. My mother and father would have chided me for my lack of table manners and the layer of dirt covering every inch of me. I smiled. There was something alluring about knowing that the human family who had always seemed to put up with me rather than love me would be horrified about how I was acting. I wondered what they were doing right now. Especially Rose.

A pang of sadness filled my chest, which surprised me. Rose and I never got along, but I expected that she'd be a part of my life forever. It was strange knowing that I wouldn't see her get married or meet her children. Suddenly, I felt detached and alone.

"Is everything alright?" Ethan asked.

I forced a smile. "I'm fine. Just tired."

He popped a bite of food into his mouth and chewed slowly while he studied me. After swallowing, he shook his head. "It's more than that."

I shrugged.

"Leave her alone, Ethan," Cormac said. "Not everyone wants to talk about how they feel."

Grateful for Cormac's words, I ate in silence. My appetite was gone, but I forced myself to finish the apple, knowing I'd need the food before we left for the next part of our journey.

Setting the core down on the table, I looked up at Cormac. "Can you show me where I can sleep?"

He rose and the others stood as well, moving away from the table to follow him. Right then, I just wanted to be alone and I didn't like the idea of them all walking me to a bedroom. I didn't complain, though. If the end result was that I got some alone time to clear my head, it was worth it.

Cormac led me up the stairs, Dane and Ethan trailed behind us. The small staircase shook with each step and I wondered if it could support all of our weight at once.

At the top of the stairs there was a short hallway with a door on either side. Cormac opened the nearest door. "You can sleep here."

"Thank you," I said, moving closer to the open door.

"I'll join you," Dane said.

"I can sleep by myself, thanks," I said.

"It's not safe, love. You smell like magic and honeysuckle. The creatures'll come right for you," Dane said, sliding closer to me.

"Cormac?" I turned to him, seeking an ally.

Cormac's brow furrowed and his lips turned down in a slight frown. "Dane's right. They'll smell you from a mile away."

My mouth dropped open in surprise. Cormac was usually unconcerned about me despite his announcement that I was under his protection at the wedding. "It's not necessary."

"No argument, Cassia." Cormac's eyes made contact with mine and I saw nothing but detached resolve. Not even a flicker of the connection we'd forged over the last few days.

I scowled, crossing my arms over my chest. I wanted to stomp my foot and yell at him, but I wasn't a child. And these princes had been doing everything they could to keep me alive. If they thought having one of them in my room would help keep the monsters away, I needed to follow along. "Fine."

Cormac broke eye contact and turned to Dane and Ethan. "One of you, in her bed." He turned and walked away, then paused in front of one of the rooms but didn't turn back. "Sleep. If the rumors about the monsters near the falls are true, you'll all need to be rested."

My face heated. What else did he expect we'd be doing in the room if we weren't sleeping?

"I'll do it," Dane said.

"I'm sure you would," Ethan said. "But I'm going to take this round."

"Why you?" Dane asked.

"Because I'm a gentleman," Ethan said.

"You just pretend to be a gentleman," Dane said. "I've seen you at the Harvest Ball."

"How about we let Cassia decide?" I asked.

Both Fae cleared their throats and turned to me, then gave an incline of their heads.

"That's fair," Ethan said.

"More than fair," Dane said.

"Sleep only," I said.

"Sleep only," Dane said, covering his heart with his hand.

"Agree," Ethan said.

I took a step toward Ethan and pulled on the collar of his blood stained tunic to peek at the healing wound. It wasn't open anymore, his magic had healed him well, but it was still an angry red slash across his shoulder.

I remembered how tired the healing process made me and let out a sigh. "Ethan, you need more rest. That needs to finish healing."

"I'm fine, I assure you," he said, covering my hand with his so it was pressed against his firm chest.

"I know you are, but I need to know you're recovering. You focus on taking care of yourself tonight." I glanced at Dane before looking back at Ethan. "I'm sure Dane will be a perfect gentleman."

Chapter Twenty-Three

I walked into the room and tried not to let the fact that Dane was going to be staying the night in the same room as me get to me. The door shut behind me and I could feel the presence of another person even though I wasn't looking at him.

Even when I was a young child, I had slept in my own room. When I was very young, I remember Nani occasionally sleeping on the floor near my bed if I had nightmares. But when I woke in the morning, she was never there. So I knew she just stayed for a short time and then went to her own sleeping quarters.

It was strange to know that someone else was in there with me. I looked around the room and felt my chest tighten at the sight of the small bed that took up most of the space. It would be difficult to even find enough floor space to stretch out on for a normal person, not to mention someone as tall and broad as Dane. The bed might even be too short for him, but it was wide enough for two people. My cheeks heated when I realized the only logical sleeping arrangement would be for the two of us to share the bed.

I turned around to ask Dane what he thought and let out a squeak of surprise.

Dane froze halfway through removing one of the legs of his trousers.

"What are you doing?" I asked.

"You don't expect me to sleep in these filthy clothes, do you?" he asked.

I stared at him, my mouth hanging open, as I tried to think of something to say. He finished removing his trousers and when he dropped them to the floor, a cloud of dust rose from them.

I had to concede that he was right, our clothes were filthy. As much as I didn't want to sleep in the dust from the road, I wasn't sure I was ready to sleep naked next to Dane.

"Surely you've seen men without their clothes on," Dane said as he lifted his tunic over his head.

I stared at him, blinking in silence, taking in every inch of his bare chest. From the firm chest muscles to the rippling muscles of his abdomen and finally, pausing at the V shaped indent of his hips. Thankfully, he was still wearing some undergarments to cover the lower portion. Yet, I found myself curious to know what he looked like completely naked.

"I've never been with a man. Remember you met me on my wedding day. Nothing really happened after that," I said.

"I forget," he said with a knowing smile, "you humans don't let yourself have very much fun."

"You're the ones who keep saying I'm not human. It's very confusing when you keep lumping me in with them," I said, feeling frustrated.

The longer I stayed in Faerie, the more comfortable I felt. But in these moments, where one of the princes referred to me as human, it set me right back to the place of doubt and denial. I felt like I was trapped between the two realms, and uncomfortably living in neither. It was an awful way to feel. I had moments where I felt free and safe here. Then, something would happen to pull me right out of that newfound comfort.

"You're right," Dane said taking a step toward me. "You're not human. Which means, you don't have to follow the rules if you don't want to."

My pulse raced, quickening with each step Dane took toward me. He stopped just in front of me, close enough that he could lean in and our bodies would press together. But he didn't, he was waiting.

I looked up at him, fixing my gaze on his sparkling blue eyes. He was pure masculinity and raw sexuality all rolled together. My breathing grew shallow and I felt tingling begin in my breasts that trailed down to between my legs.

Curiosity winning over the morals I had been taught as a human, I lifted my hands and placed my palms on Dane's bulging chest then ran my fingertips over the rippling muscles of his stomach down to his bellybutton. I pulled my hands away and Dane caught my wrist, gently tugging me closer to him.

He leaned in and I could feel his hot breath on my neck as his lips brushed against my earlobe. "We don't have to do anything you don't want to do. But just so you know, I'm happy to do anything you ask of me."

He kissed my neck, pressing soft lips against the sensitive skin. Goosebumps trailed down my arms and a thrill shot through me. I gasped, breathing in his rosemary and honey scent as he softly kissed me again.

I moaned as his lips trailed down to my shoulder. Slowly, Dane moved the fabric of my tunic aside. Then he stopped, and straightened and stared back down at me. His eyes looked different now, hungry somehow, and his shallow breaths matched my own.

We stared at each other for a moment, neither of us speaking. Then, slowly, Dane reached for the lacing on my tunic and tugged at the cord, unraveling the knot.

He lowered his hand, and waited. It was as if he were giving me time to stop him or turn away from him. Or maybe he was unsure of this himself. I didn't want to stop, desire flooded through my brain, making me feel fuzzy. All I could think of was the feel of his skin beneath my fingers and his lips pressed against mine. In one fluid movement, I lifted the tunic over my head and tossed it aside. Dane didn't hesitate, before the tunic even hit the ground, he scooped me up and carried me over to the bed.

His lips pressed against my neck again and continued to trail around my throat and down to my chest. He paused again and looked up at me.

"Don't stop," I said.

That was all he needed, confirmation. He tore off my undergarments tossing them to the ground. His lips moved to my breasts, his tongue tracing over my sensitive nipples.

He cupped them with his hands and let out a moan of approval, then returned his mouth to explore my body more.

I threw my head back, letting out a moan of my own as feelings of pleasure washed through me. Dane climbed on top of me, straddling me. I could feel his stiff erection rubbing against my thigh as he leaned down and pressed his lips to mine.

I expected him to push hard, but he was gentle and his lips were soft against mine. He moved his mouth helping me find a rhythm with his lips before falling back just enough to lick my lower lip. I shivered and gasped just as he pressed his mouth back to mine.

Dane ran his fingers through my hair and lowered his hands to my shoulders and in a quick movement, rolled me on top of him.

Now I was the one straddling him, looking down at his perfect body. My long blonde hair fell in waves cascading over my breasts. He toyed with the ends for a moment lazily, before wrapping his arms around my back and pulling me down to him. My breasts pressed into his chest and he kissed me again. This time, there was more urgency in the kiss and he pulled me closer as he pressed his lips to mine.

I broke away from the kiss, gasping for air. My whole body felt like it was on fire. I felt alive, but I knew if I kept going, I wasn't going to stop. I sat up and looked down at the Fae Prince under me, breathing heavy.

Dane reached his hand up and brushed his fingertips across my cheek. "I think ruining your wedding day might just be the best thing that's ever happened to me."

I leaned down and gave him a quick kiss on the lips and climbed off of him. "You know, I thought it was going to be the worst day of my life, and now I wouldn't trade it for anything." I lay down next to him and rested my head on his shoulder. He pulled his arm out so he could hold me and I repositioned myself on his chest.

"Can we just lay like this?" I asked.

He kissed my forehead and brushed the loose strands of hair away from my eyes. "Of course." He kissed my forehead again. "Get some rest. You're safe here."

Chapter Twenty-Four

Warm sunlight filtered in the small window of the tiny room. Dane had his arms wrapped around me, his strong chest against my back. Careful so I didn't wake him, I squirmed out from between his arms and I sat on the edge of the bed thinking about the feel of his lips against mine last night.

I knew there was more to sex than kissing and touching, and I was curious about it, but it was hard to distance myself from my upbringing. Though, I had to admit, if sex was even better than what I had done with Dane last night, I had a hard time seeing why it wasn't something that was talked about more. What we did last night made me feel amazing, it made me feel alive. What could be so wrong with it?

I walked over to where my torn undergarments lay on the pile on the floor. I picked them up and examined them. They were unusable, so I tossed them aside before throwing my tunic over my head. Behind me, Dane snored softly, and I covered my mouth to keep from letting my giggle wake him.

On tip toes, I crept toward the door and quietly opened it before closing it behind me. I heard voices downstairs, and followed the sound to the tiny main living area. Cormac and Ethan were sitting at the table, each with a cup of small ale.

"Good morning," Ethan said, sliding a cup to an empty place at the table. I sat down in front of the cup as he filled it with amber liquid.

"Did you have a restful evening?" he asked.

I took a sip from my cup then scrunched up my nose in response to the bitter taste before setting it back down. "Yes, thank you."

"I told you Dane could go a night without bedding a female in the same room," Ethan said.

"Then why is it that she smells like him?" Cormac asked.

"Maybe she smells like him because she shared a bed with him last night. And what she did or didn't do is none of your business," I said.

Cormac grumbled something about getting the horses ready and left the table.

"Nice to see you standing up for yourself to him," Ethan said. "Aside from Dane and myself, most people just agree with him."

"I understand," I said. "But aren't you all royalty? Is Cormac in charge?" I asked.

"Sort of," Ethan said. "The current Queen hails from the Autumn Court, so the Autumn Court is currently the high court. If the Queen were from the Summer Court, then people would react that way to Dane."

"How do you keep it all straight?" I asked.

"Well, we do study at the Academy. Plus, when you've been alive as long as we all have, you pick up a thing or two."

I thought about asking how old they all were, but it didn't seem relevant. If you live forever, did age even matter?

"You found ale," Dane's voice came from behind me.

I felt my cheeks heat and kept my eyes on the cup in front of me.

Dane sat down in the chair next to me. "Good morning, love."

"Morning," I said, risking a glance upward.

Ethan was staring at me, one eyebrow raised in a knowing way. I looked away from him again. I didn't owe Ethan anything, but now that I thought about it, Ethan was the kindest of my companions. He was gentle and sweet. If I were to choose one of them to be my first, Ethan made the most sense. The thought sent blood rushing to my cheeks and to the place between my legs.

I passed my cup to Dane. "You can have mine. I'm going to get ready."

Neither of them said a word to me as I darted away from the table back toward the rooms upstairs.

After a few minutes of cleaning myself up as best I could in the foggy looking glass in the bathroom, I walked back downstairs. Dane and Ethan were still sitting at the table.

"Cormac still outside?" I asked.

"I think so," Ethan said.

"I'll go see if he needs any help." I rushed away before either of them could say anything. I wasn't sure what I expected or why I felt so out of sorts.

Dane was strong, and funny, and looked out for me. He had all of the protective aspects I'd longed for in a mate, yet, the longer I spent there, the more I realized I could take care of myself. But that wasn't what was upsetting me. I just couldn't pinpoint what it was that made me feel so guilty about my time with Dane. It seemed more than just my upbringing at work.

As I neared the stables, I caught sight of Cormac as he tightened a saddle on his horse. Mine was already saddled, which meant Cormac had taken care of Starlight for me before he got around to his own work. My chest tightened and suddenly I realized why I felt the way I did. It wasn't that I felt guilty for being with Dane, I felt like I was betraying Cormac and Ethan. It didn't make any sense, but in such a short time, I felt a connection to all three of them that made me want to run to each of them. Was this normal? Would I have felt this way if I'd seen three attractive human males in the mortal realm? Maybe it was their Fae blood. Or mine. Maybe it was something else entirely.

A twig snapped under my step and Cormac glanced up. "Did you eat?"

I paused and looked at him, my brow furrowing in confusion. "What?"

"Did you eat? You didn't seem to like the ale," he said.

I shook my head. "I'm fine."

He finished tightening the saddle and patted his horse before walking over to me. He pulled something out of the pouch on his hip and handed it to me. "You need to eat. You didn't eat much last night and I'm sure you worked up an appetite after spending the night with Dane."

"What's that supposed to mean?" I asked, taking the bundle of cloth from his hands.

"Nothing, that's not my business," he said.

I narrowed my eyes. "Are you jealous?"

"Of course not," he said. "Eat."

Frowning, I looked down at the bundle in my hands and pulled away the fabric to reveal a small loaf of brown bread. I broke it in half and steam rose from the loaf. It was still warm in the middle. The smell of fresh yeast and flour made my stomach grumble. "Where did you get this?"

He shrugged. "Couldn't sleep this morning so I found a bakery."

I knew there was nothing nearby, but I was too hungry to question the gift. I walked over to Cormac and handed him half. "Thank you."

"You eat it," he said.

"I don't need it all," I said.

"Then save some for later," he said.

Again, I extended the bread toward him.

He shook his head.

Knowing how stubborn he was, I decided I should concede. I could always give it to him later. Carefully, I wrapped the other half back in the cloth. "Thank you."

"I meant what I said, Cassia," he said. "I will protect you. We all will." He lifted his chin, indicating something behind me and I turned to see Dane and Ethan walking toward us.

"All cleaned up in the house," Ethan said.

"Ready when you are," Dane said. "Let's go hunt some monsters."

⚜

MY THIGHS BURNED in protest as once again, we rode through the endless countryside. As much as I enjoyed riding Starlight, I found myself longing to stay put in the same place for more than one night. Though, I wasn't sure that I'd be granted that wish even once this was over. It was hard to picture a future that was so uncertain.

True to his word, the ride to the village of Twin Falls was short. It was still morning when we arrived. The warm sunshine and a touch of crisp Autumn air greeted us as we entered the sleepy village.

Twin Falls was a sleepy village nestled in a valley surrounded by trees. I could see why people liked living there. It was peaceful and cooler than it had been on the open road. Birdsong filled the morning air as I stepped onto some soft dew covered grass. I wondered if I could possibly settle down in one of these little villages and barter for room and board. Maybe when this was done, I'd ride back to a place like this.

We stopped in front of an inn and Cormac led my horse and his away while Ethan did the same with his and Dane's horse. Leaving Dane and me alone for the first time since last night.

"Did I do something to upset you?" Dane asked.

"No," I said. "I enjoyed our time. It's just hard to get used to how different things are here."

"Did it feel wrong?" Dane asked gently.

"No." I hadn't stopped to think about that and blurted the word out before I really let the question sink in. But it was the truth. Being around Dane felt right; being around all of the princes felt right.

Before we could go any farther with our conversation, Cormac and Ethan returned.

"I just want to meet with our source before we head into the forest," Cormac said.

We followed him toward a pub with a faded green dragon on a sign that hung precariously by one of its two hooks. The dragon on the sign, much like the exterior of the building, looked like it had once been crafted from a place of great care and fallen into disrepair over the years.

"This way." Cormac pushed open the door and Ethan followed him, holding the door open for me to enter. I went through after hesitating at the threshold for a moment. This didn't seem like the type of place that was safe to be stopping in. Quickly, I reminded myself that I wasn't alone and I wasn't in the company of humans who would abandon me at the first sign of trouble.

The inside of the bar smelled like pipe weed, sweat, and ale. It was a combination of every smell I disliked that seemed to cling to so many men. I fought the urge to wrinkle my nose in disgust and instead pressed my lips together and tried my best to maintain a neutral expression.

The pub was dark and empty this early in the morning as none of the window shutters had been open. I wondered if they ever opened them and let in the sunlight and I worried about what I would see on the floor or the tables if they ever did. As it was, my boots stuck to the floor as I walked and I had a feeling the same sticky substance covering the floor was probably on every flat surface.

A pair of double doors behind a shiny maple bar top swung

open and a creature of at least eight feet tall with wide bulging eyes and gray, pallid skin walked through. He smiled, showing long yellow teeth that crowded his mouth so much, I wondered how he had room for them all. The creature took heavy footsteps toward our group then extended his arms as he reached Cormac embracing him in a monstrous hug.

"Cormac, it's been too long," the creature said.

"Levin, it's good to see you. Thank you for sending that information our way."

"Of course, those creatures are scaring away business. Can't feed my family with an empty pub and everyone's afraid to go out at night for fear of being attacked," Levin said.

"How many creatures have come into the village?" Dane asked.

"We've had six attacks so far. And the weird part is they're traveling in packs. Never seen that before," Levin said, then he turned to look at me. "Which one of you finally bagged a girl? And why the hell are you crazy enough to bring her along hunting Sodalis?"

"This is Cassia, she's helping us," Dane said.

"I'm sure she's very helpful," Levin said with a wink.

I frowned and bit down on the inside of my cheek to keep from commenting. Levin wasn't a creature anyone should mess with. He clearly wasn't human and he didn't look anything like the Fae princes or any other Fae I'd met so far. I wasn't sure what he was, but he was big and intimidating.

"Don't let that pretty face fool you, Levin," Dane said. "She's already killed a few of the beasts."

Levin raised his brows. "Really? I won't even go after those creatures. They're disgusting."

"They really are," I said. "I think I'll be washing Sodalis blood and drool off of me for the next month."

Levin howled with laugher. "I like this one, Dane. I think you should keep her."

Chapter Twenty-Five

"When was the last attack?" Cormac asked.

"Two days ago," Levin said.

"And they wait until nightfall?" Ethan asked.

Levin nodded. "It's not typical. They don't usually stick around like this and they never travel in packs."

"And it came from the North?" Cormac said.

Levin nodded again. "We're guessing they're staying somewhere near the falls. But since they're traveling in groups now, none of the fighters here are willing to go into the woods after them. We don't exactly know how many there are. Could be the same group attacking or it could be sending out hunting parties to collect fresh meat every few days."

I shuddered at the thought of the whole herd of the monsters organizing enough to send out hunting parties to return back to a massive number of them.

"Thank you for your help, Levin. We'll take care of them."

"Anything I can get you before you head out?" Levin asked.

"We could use a small restock of rations, just in case it takes longer than a day," Cormac said.

Five minutes later, we were out the door with a bundle of food and a mission: Find the creatures, and as Cormac promised, take care of them.

As we rode away from town, I rode up alongside Cormac. "What are we expected to do? Smell them out?"

"That's one way. As you notice, they had a very distinct scent," Cormac said.

I meant the words sarcastically, but Cormac apparently didn't notice or didn't care.

"You said you'd help teach me how to do this." I knew Cormac wasn't great at answering questions, but this was something he might agree to follow through on and I was eager to learn anything I could.

"Lesson begins once we get out of town," Cormac said.

Several minutes after we had passed the last building on the edge of Twin Falls Village, we were still riding in silence. I was about to ask him what I should be doing when Cormac suddenly halted his progress. Starlight stopped next to his horse.

"Tracking is about using your senses," Cormac said. "All of your senses. Smell, when it comes to creatures such as these can be a powerful ally. There's also sight, sound, taste, and your intuition. Don't ignore that little voice inside that tells you not to overlook something or to turn in a different direction. All great trackers have it and it can mean the difference between life and death. But you can't only follow your intuition. It needs to work in concert with the rest, a symbiotic relationship of the things you experience coupled with the things you feel."

I nodded and took a deep breath, trying to take it all in. It seemed a little unbelievable that in addition to just looking for things, I could find an inner voice to give me clues. I wasn't sure I had something like that. I had a feeling, I was going to have to rely on my senses. Wanting to show Cormac that I was taking it seriously, that I could learn, I looked around us. We were on another dirt road, once again lined by trees. The Autumn Court seemed to be mostly made of woods and forests.

The trees swayed musically in the wind, leaves mimicking the sound of rain. I took a deep breath, expecting to smell nothing but grass and dirt but was surprised that I caught the tail end of the scent of death. It was the smell of the Sodalis, and I found my mind assaulted with images of blood, sharp claws, and snapping jaws.

I wrinkled my nose and opened my eyes then shook the vision from my head. My stomach twisted at the thought of facing the monsters down again.

"What is it?" Cormac asked.

Pushing the fear away, I turned toward the scent and noticed more details. "The tree branches, they're broken. The grass is matted. Something large came through right there."

"And?" Cormac asked.

"I can smell them," I said.

"And what do you think we should do, little tracker?" Cormac asked.

Something inside me told me that following them there would not give me the results I was looking for. A flicker of fear signaled danger, but that didn't make sense. Wasn't that what we were there to do? Follow the creatures and find them?

"Trust your instincts, Cassia. What do you think we should do?" Cormac asked.

"We can't go in through that way," I said.

"Why not?" Cormac asked.

"I'm not sure, but it doesn't feel safe."

Cormac smiled. "Perhaps you would be a good candidate for tracking at the Academy. You're right, entering through that small path could be dangerous. We could be trapped in the under-growth and the horses won't make it through. If the creatures are hidden, they could attack us before we even saw them. We have to find another way that gives us the advantage. At least now we know they're near," Cormac said.

"We'll take the bridge to the other side of the river. If they're anything like the other creatures we've hunted, they don't like being too far from water. The closer we get to the falls, the more likely we are to run into them."

As we continued down the road toward the bridge, the smell of the monsters grew stronger. By the time we crossed the bridge, I pulled my tunic up over my face to try to filter out some of the stench. We had to be close and I wasn't sure I wanted to know how many of the beasts we would find if they were letting off that strong of a smell when we couldn't even see them yet.

I continued to scan the undergrowth and trees for any signs of disruption. My heart hammered in my chest partly due to anticipation, partly due to fear. I didn't want one of these creatures to sneak up on me, that had happened too many times already. Fiery red and orange leaves of the trees wrestled with the wind, but other than that, I couldn't hear any sound in the forest.

"Do you think they're sleeping?" I asked.

"It's possible, he did say they've been coming out at night."

Cormac stopped riding and lifted his fist into the air, signaling for the rest of us to stop. I held my breath as I looked around for any sign of what made him decide that this was where we needed to wait.

I didn't have to look too hard, in front of us was a massive patch of flattened moss and grass littered with broken tree branches and bones. I saw a patch of what looked to be human hair and gagged, swallowing down the bile that rose up in my throat as I turned away. The creatures weren't here anymore, but they'd been here.

Cormac dismounted and Ethan walked up from behind us. I noticed Dane was holding the reins of both his horse and Ethan's while Ethan took hold of Cormac's horse so he could go exploring.

"Come on down, maybe learn something," Cormac said to me.

I dismounted, nearly landing on my face in the process, and handed my reins over to Ethan. Wordlessly, I joined Cormac stepping around the piles of bones and matted fur. Flies buzzed over the carcasses that had been left behind and I swatted them away as I walked through. My stomach churned and I hoped I'd be able to refrain from getting sick all over Cormac's boots.

Cormac walked to the edge of the matted grass and crouched low. I joined him, copying his movements. From this vantage point, I noticed there was a tunnel through the underbrush, between the trees, that seemed to go on for quite a distance.

Low hanging branches around the tunnel were broken and stomped on as if the creatures fled from this space to another.

The part of the woods they headed into was thick with trees and shrubs and would be impossible for horses to pass through. I stood and weaved in between a few of the trees to get a closer view. Cormac grabbed my hand and pulled me back. "You can't go that way."

I pulled my arm away from his grasp and stared off into the distance. The trees beyond this growth looked different than the rest of the woods. The fiery leaves were gone, replaced by fields of green.

"What is that place?" I asked. It was clear there was a change there. Something shifted with the disappearance of the trees I'd grown accustomed to in the Autumn Court. It was as if some invisible divider separated these woods from another place. It was unfamiliar, yet part of me felt a pull toward the new trees.

"We're at the border," Cormac said. "Beyond the Autumn trees is the Winter Court. We can't pass through that."

"But the creatures can?" I asked.

"We have no jurisdiction there, we signed the treaty. We can't violate it," Cormac said. "Sodalis don't worry about treaties."

"And even if we wanted to," Dane said. "None of us can pass through that barrier. Only the Fae with winter blood can get through. For the rest of us." Dane made a slicing motion with his finger across his throat.

"So how do we finish this? How do we get rid of these

monsters and keep them from attacking me?" If the creatures were taking sanctuary in the Winter Court, did that mean they knew we were hunting them? Were they there biding their time until the princes left me alone so I would be unprotected? "How do we close the tear?"

"The only way the monsters can travel into the Winter Court is if the tear is in that court. The barrier should have kept them out," Dane said.

"Well there's a ruler there, right?" I asked. "Surely there's a way to communicate the importance of this."

"There's a prince there," Ethan said. "But he doesn't take kindly to visitors. We have to do this the right way, through official channels."

"What's to stop them from coming back then?" I asked. "I'm tired of constantly worrying that I'm going to be mauled to death. Do you think they will stay there? That they're done coming after me?" I asked.

All three princes were silent, but I could read their expressions. Even Dane, who usually wore a face of confidence, looked crestfallen.

"How do we send the message to the Winter Court?" I asked.

"We have to go to the border crossing," Cormac said. Without any other explanation, he mounted his horse. "Back to town. We'll have to slide there."

Chapter Twenty-Six

I was surprised when Cormac led us right back to the stables in town. I thought the stable master was surprised, too. But he was happy to accept the coin Cormac offered in exchange for housing our horses.

"Is it that far away?" I asked. Hadn't we just been at the border for the Winter Court? I wondered why it was that we would need to use the strange and slightly uncomfortable process to travel from where we were to where we were going.

"We border the Winter Court, that entry point is at the southernmost tip of both of our lands. It's easily a full day's ride from here to there."

"But that makes no sense, why not just go in where we were? The creatures are sneaking in at that point, we're wasting time."

"This is more than just hunting monsters. This is politics. I'm not going to start a war over this," Cormac said.

"It would be that big of a deal if another Fae crossed the border?" I asked.

"I already told you, none of us would be able to cross even if we wanted to. You have to have Winter Court blood to even be allowed through. The only way we will get a chance to talk to someone is if we enter through proper channels." Cormac paused, a frown on his lips. "I wish we could just leave you here. The Winter Court isn't a place we should take someone like you."

"Someone like me?" The words stung. I thought we were finally starting to understand each other and that I had gained at least a little bit of respect from Cormac and the other princes.

"I'm sure Cassia can take care of herself just fine," Dane said.

I smiled at him, grateful that someone was stepping up to defend me. "I've already demonstrated that I can be useful. I helped you find their tunnel and I saved your life."

"It's not that. It's Tristan, the Prince of the Winter Court. He has a reputation and I'm not sure how much of it is true," Cormac said. "I don't want anything bad to happen to you."

"Well, based on his reputation, having her there to speak for us might be beneficial," Ethan said.

"I'm not going to parade Cassia in front of someone like him," Dane said.

"I'm going with you, you know I attract those creatures and if you leave me here they'll just come back. We're wasting time standing here," I said.

"She does have a point," Dane said, winking at me.

"Fine, don't let go," Cormac said as he embraced me with his strong arms.

I buried my face into his chest and squeezed him tighter than I needed to in anticipation of the strange sensation I knew was coming. I wasn't a fan of traveling like this, but if this was the way to seal the tear between realms and put an end to those creatures hunting me, I was willing to do whatever I needed to. Including speaking to some depraved prince of a forbidden court.

I felt the pull low in the pit of my stomach as I was submerged in total darkness. Sounds and air seemed to be sucked away from me as if I'd entered a vacuum. Then, just as I was starting to feel claustrophobic, my feet touched down on solid ground and I let out a breath of relief. Hoping this would be a normal means of transportation, I slowly eased up my grip around Cormac's waist. Surprisingly, he was still holding onto me. I lingered in his embrace taking a moment to breathe in the scent of citrus and cedar that I'd come to known as decidedly Cormac.

From behind us somebody cleared their throat and Cormac let go. I stepped away from him, but still felt the warmth of his touch on my skin. For just a second, I allowed myself to imagine what it would be like to do the things I'd done with Dane with Cormac. I wondered if underneath that tough exterior was a gentle lover or if his kisses would feel just as powerful as him.

"The place hasn't changed much," Ethan said.

I turned and saw that we were in a grassy clearing. The landscape around me was flat and almost barren. Yellow and faded green grass was the only sign of life as far as the eye could see. It was eerie and calm and I couldn't quite put my finger on what made me so uncomfortable. Then I realized, it wasn't just a lack of life that disturbed me, it was the lack of anything. There was no wind here, no movement across the grass, no rustling of clothing from a cool breeze. I took a breath, half expecting the air to be absent, but my chest filled just as it would anywhere else. But I knew there was something different about this place. "What is this?"

"Neutral territory," Cormac said.

"The Winter Court attempted to overthrow the Queen and take control of all the courts 200 years ago. In the end, they lost the war, but gained their sovereignty. The King is gone, some say he still lives in a tower of his castle and is completely mad, or he's dead. So the Prince rules in his absence," Ethan said.

"Most of us think the son is probably mad too," Dane said.

"Whatever he is, he's not someone you want to cross. He has a reputation for violence and an appetite for the unusual. The sooner we can get this over with, the better," Cormac said.

I was second-guessing my choice to come along and I swallowed a lump in my throat as I stared into the void of nothing. I half expected an entryway, gate, or an archway that could signify a separation between the two courts. I hadn't expected to be standing in the middle of a field. "Now what?"

"We wait, they know we're here by now. It shouldn't be too long," Cormac said.

I closed my eyes and tried to think about what it might be like when this was over. No more monsters chasing me, no more fear. We were so close to finishing this quest. The Winter Prince had to understand the danger these creatures were and had to agree to let the princes seal the tear. Enemy or not, there was no way I would want these loose in my kingdom if I were in charge.

The back of my neck tingled and I turned on instinct. My blood went cold. A whole herd of Sodalis were running toward us. For a monster that didn't usually travel in packs, they sure seemed to unite when it came to finding me.

Cormac and Dane drew their swords and Ethan readied his bow. My heartbeat pounded in my ears blocking out any noise the beasts made as they approached. I tensed, unsure of what to do. The little bit of magic I had was unreliable and wouldn't be able to stop this many monsters. My eyes darted across the creatures, counting them. A fresh wave of terror washed through me as I reached twenty.

We'd seen smaller groups and the princes had bested them. But what chance did any of them have against this many? We had to get out of here. We could clear some distance from them and then slide back to town. Anything to prevent the bloody face off that would result in taking on this many creatures at once.

I stepped back, away from the onslaught. My chest rose and fell in rapid succession and I felt like I wasn't getting enough air.

Ethan looked back at me and his eyes widened. "Cassia, no. Don't go that way."

I heard his words, but I continued to move backward, as if drawn away by some unseen force.

Ethan lowered his bow and reached for me, then stopped

suddenly. He turned and said something to Cormac, but I couldn't hear him even though I could see his mouth moving.

Cormac and Dane both turned to face me and looked around not making eye contact with me.

I waved my hands, trying to show them where I was, to let them know I was safe, but it was as if they couldn't see me.

"They can't see you," a male voice said. The sound slithered over my skin like silk.

I turned around and found myself face to face with a Fae male. He was head and shoulders taller than me, just like the princes. Though, this male was different. His icy blue eyes studied me like a hunter stares down their prey. His features were sharp and angular. He wore a smile, complete with pointed canines on clear display. The only thing soft about him was the bun of sun kissed blonde hair on top of his head. "Welcome to the Winter Court."

Chapter Twenty-Seven

I looked around and realized I was no longer in the endless expanse of grass. I was in a courtyard made of white stone. Arches and columns rose around us, boxing us in. I shivered. It was much colder there than it had been in the Autumn Court and I wasn't dressed for winter.

"I have to get back there," I said. "My friends are in danger. I have to help them. Please. Tell me how to get back."

The stranger narrowed his eyes. "Why are you traveling with all three of the princes of Faerie?"

"We're hunting the monsters," I said, desperation tugging at my voice. "And they were closing in on my friends. I have to get back there."

"I thought I knew all of the Winter Fae, but somehow, I missed getting to know you," the male said. "Were you raised in a different court?"

"I'm not a Winter Fae," I said, doubting the words as I spoke them. I didn't know what I was. It was just as likely that I was a Winter Fae, I supposed. Angela had suggested it was possible, but the princes seemed to think it so unlikely that a Winter Fae would be left in the human world that I'd ignored that possibility.

"If you're not a Winter Fae, how did you get through my wards?" he asked.

I turned around, hoping to see them but they were gone from sight. Either I couldn't see them through the invisible barrier I'd crossed or they had slid back to town. Somehow I doubted that was the case. I had a feeling they were facing down against the creatures as we stood here wasting time.

I swallowed and looked back at the handsome stranger. He didn't have the same calming effect that the three princes had on me. If anything, he was the opposite. My skin tingled and flutters filled my chest. This Fae was dangerous. Every part of me was sending off warnings. I knew I should turn and go back the way I came, but I stayed rooted to the spot. As much as he scared me, he also intrigued me. "Please, show me how to get back there."

"Why were you waiting with the queen's errand boys?" he asked.

I glared at him. Cormac, Dane, and Ethan were nobody's errand boys. They were strong and kind and wonderful. And they were princes in their own right. Even if I didn't understand the court politics of Faerie, I knew this was an insult. But they were in danger and they needed my help. "We have a message for the Winter Court prince. And if you're not going to help me, just show me how to get back."

The male crossed his arms over his chest and cocked his head to the side. "What's the message?"

I narrowed my eyes at him. "You're the prince, aren't you?"

"Who else would I be?" he asked.

"I don't know, a guard?" I looked around and realized that we were alone in this strange enclosed space.

"This is my meeting space," the prince explained. "I take my guests here. There's no magic allowed within these walls." He gestured to the white stone. "What's your message?"

"You're really just going to stand here while Cormac, Dane, and Ethan are in danger?" I asked, shaking my head.

He lifted an amused eyebrow.

I let out an annoyed huff, then took a deep breath. "We were tracking some monsters, Sodalis, from the Under."

"I know what a Sodalis is and I know what the Under is," he said. "But something tells me, you're not as familiar with it."

I ignored him. "We tracked them to your court. We think the tear between realms is here and we need to close it."

"Tristan, by the way," he said.

My brow furrowed.

"My name is Tristan. And yours is?" he asked.

"Cassia," I said. "Now, please, can you either send me back there or help us?"

"And you are part of this because?" Tristan asked.

My stomach twisted as I wondered what was happening to my friends while I stood here wasting time with this cocky prince. "Does it matter?"

He nodded.

"Fine," I said. "The monsters seem to be chasing me. Angela said she thinks they're coming after me and that more will keep coming until we seal the tear."

"Angela? Cormac's Angela?" Tristan asked.

I hesitated, wondering if I was betraying Cormac by answering the question. Perhaps I shouldn't have even mentioned Angela at all. Deciding I'd already said it, I nodded.

Tristan pursed his lips and drummed his fingers on his arm. "What's in it for me?"

"Seriously?" I asked. "You can't want these things loose in your court and you can't be so evil that you'll let three Fae get eaten by monsters while you stood by and did nothing."

"Oh, I don't care about your friends, but you're right, I don't want those monsters in my court. But you already told me they're after you. So they aren't going to harm me or the members of my court as long as they're chasing you," he said. "But you have everything to lose if I don't help you."

"I don't have anything," I said. "Please, we just need help fighting these creatures and entering your court long enough to hunt the monsters and seal the tear. Then they'll leave," I said.

"We haven't had an outsider in this court since the war. I'm not interested in letting three princes in just before the Queen's Trial starts. I might not be part of the ordeal, but I know the invitations went out yesterday."

"What would this have to do with the Queen's Trial?" I asked.

"Well, I assume since you're running around with them, that you four must have your sights set on the throne," he said.

"I assure you, that's not what I'm here for," I said.

"Prove it," he said.

I bit down on my lower lip, trying to think of anything I could say that might demonstrate the need for him to help us aside from giving away my secret. I didn't know enough about the Queen's Trial or why my being there would make him think I wanted to win.

"If you're not interested in sharing, I'm not sure I can help you." He waved his hand lazily in front of me, then turned away.

"Wait," I called out after him. "You're right. I'm new to the whole idea of the Under and the creatures that live there. I'm new to all of it. Queen's Trial, courts, princes, everything. I just got here a few days ago. This is all new to me."

Tristan stopped walking and pivoted to face me. "And how is that possible? Especially for one who clearly has the blood of the Winter Court."

"I'm a changeling," I said. "I was raised in the human realm. Cormac, Dane, and Ethan found me when they followed a Sodalis into the human world."

Tristan moved closer to me then leaned down so his face was level with mine. He stared at me a long time, his eyes locked on mine as if trying to see inside my head. I wondered if what Angela said was true about the Winter Fae. Could they see the future? If this was true, what did this male see for me?

Finally, Tristan stood. "I'll help you. But I'll need something in return."

"What?" I asked. "I told you, I have nothing."

"I want to know everything you know about the human realm," he said.

I replayed his words over and over in my mind, trying to find the way he was tricking me. It seemed like too simple of a request. "That's it? I share my knowledge with you about the human realm and you help us so they can finish this?"

He nodded.

"I'll do it," I said. "Now send me back."

Tristan waved his hand in front of his face and the stone arches melted away revealing a vast grassy field. A moment later, the sounds of battle filled my ears. I turned to see my princes surrounded by snarling Sodalis.

Several dead monsters lay on the ground while a few others paced in a circle around the current attack, waiting for an opening to strike.

I didn't even have time to think of a strategy to help before the waiting beasts turned toward me. As the three Sodalis charged me, terror seized me and I froze. This was what I wanted, wasn't it? To go back and help my friends.

Suddenly, Tristan moved in front of me and I heard the sound of steel being drawn from its holster as he lifted a sword in front of him. He stood with his knees slightly bent, both hands on the sword. Despite the charging beasts, he seemed focused and calm.

I took a few steps backward so I wouldn't be in the way. Tristan looked back at me with a grin on his face, and winked. Then, he charged the nearest beast.

The creature reared on its hind legs, raising its clawed front legs in the air in preparation for taking down Tristan.

"Look out!" I yelled.

Tristan sank down, going under the claws and rolled under the creature. I lost sight of him for a second under the bulging fur covered chest as the wings closed in around their prey. My heart thundered in my chest and icy fear gripped me.

Then, the beast made a gurgling sound and blood poured from its mouth. The creature fell to its side and I saw the gaping wound in its stomach as Tristan emerged from under the creature. His once pristine white clothing was covered in blood. Loose strands of hair fell from his bun and he pushed them away from his face, leaving streaks of blood and goo on his forehead. He smiled at me before running after his next target.

Chapter Twenty-Eight

Horrified, I watched as the four Fae princes attacked the creatures. All four princes were skilled with their weapons. They dodged attacks, and delivered blows with ease. I'd thought we were outnumbered, without hope as the herd of the creatures neared us, but I was wrong.

Dead Sodalis littered the ground and I noticed a few large birds circling the brawl. Scavengers, waiting to pick from the carcasses. Bile rose in my throat and I swallowed it down, not wanting to show weakness in front of this new prince. Something about him made me want to put on a brave face. I wondered if it was the fact that I might belong to his court. After all, I'd crossed the barrier that only Winter Fae could pass through. What did that mean for me? Would I have to go to the Winter Court? Would I have to leave Cormac, Ethan, and Dane behind?

My chest tightened and my lower lip trembled. I couldn't leave them. Not after everything. The thought of being apart from even one of them made my heart ache in a way that threatened to break it.

Suddenly, I noticed a flash of movement out of the corner of my eye. I turned just in time to see a Sodalis racing toward me. I turned and ran, just missing the snapping jaws.

I had no weapon, no way of fighting the monster. Pumping my arms as hard as I could, I ran toward the fight, knowing my only chance was to bring the creature closer to one of the prince's swords.

Dane was the closest, but he was holding off two beasts at the same time. I changed direction, headed toward Ethan who was on top of one of the creatures pelting it with arrows at close range.

"Ethan," I cried out.

He looked up at me and I watched his expression turn hard as he lifted the bow, aiming at the monster on my tail.

I dropped to the ground and rolled away, hoping the monster wouldn't be able to change course before Ethan's arrows found it. From all fours, I looked up as the Sodalis screamed in rage, three arrows in its face.

The monster stopped its progress and looked toward me, letting out a roar. It was close enough that spit landed on my face and arms. Disgusted, I wiped my eyes off, but didn't break my focus off of the creature.

After several heartbeats, another arrow struck the monster's side and it turned away from me, charging Ethan instead of me.

I only got a moment of relief before three more creatures turned to me. Coming this close, I should have known that my scent would draw them away from the princes.

"What are you doing? Do you want to die?" a strong, clear voice called out behind me.

I sat up and was instantly scooped up into Tristan's arms. He carried me gently, like a bride. I was so surprised, I didn't know what to say or how to react.

"Wait here," he said, setting me down.

Then, he was gone. Vanished in thin air.

I was back in the stone archway. Tristan's Winter Court

meeting room. I didn't want to be in there, away from my friends. I wanted to be there for them. I wanted to help.

I charged back the way we'd come, only to find that the stone courtyard seemed to go in an endless circle. There was no way out of there.

Slumping down to the ground, I sat with my head against my knees. It was probably best I stayed out of it, anyway. Without a weapon, they'd have to keep saving me every time one of the monsters broke free of the pack. At least here, I knew I couldn't distract them.

It helped that I'd seen how well they were handling the monsters. Cormac had said that this was his job. Every time those creatures broke free of the Under, he and his friends sent them back. I wondered how much practice he'd had over the years.

I tucked my hands under my armpits to keep them warm. My breath came out in clouds as I paced back and forth in the stone courtyard. How long had it been? There was no sense of time passing in this odd place. The clouds above me didn't seem to move and I couldn't even find the sun. I wondered if this was how the Winter Court was or if all of it was some strange illusion created by Tristan. I had a feeling none of it was real. I was probably pacing through the prairie grasses, but couldn't see them.

I reached down, brushing my fingers against the stone. It felt rough to the touch, nothing unusual about it, but I knew it wasn't real. I pressed my fingers into the rock, willing it to dissolve as it had before. Nothing happened.

I stood back up and shook my head, feeling foolish. Then, that familiar clawing feeling inside my chest returned. This was the first time I'd felt it when I wasn't in a life or death situation. Fear shot through me as a horrifying idea sprung to mind. Maybe one of the princes was in trouble. Was it possible I could sense something through the barrier?

Mentally, I grabbed hold of the tiny internal threat and pulled against the clawing inside me, willing it to escape. Facing the direction I guessed was the barrier, I focused on returning the way I'd come. *Let me out*, I thought, internally screaming the words over and over. *Let me out.*

A burst of white light radiated from me and I gasped, still surprised by the magic I created. Squinting into the light I thought back to the last time I used the untrained magic. I'd made myself see through it by asking to see. *Let me see*, I thought.

Shapes began to come into view and to my surprise, I was not seeing any arches or stone walkways. Instead, I saw bodies moving around in the light.

I moved toward the shapes that I knew were my friends. As I walked toward them, I had to weave around fallen Sodalis. Thankfully, I no longer heard any growls or saw any active beasts.

As I drew nearer, my heart fell into my stomach. One of the figures was lying on the ground, three other figures standing around the fallen prince. *Let me see*, I screamed the words with such intensity that I felt the meaning of them vibrating in my soul.

With a crack, the light dissipated, leaving me blinking into the sunlight of the grassy field.

Three heads turned to look at me and I looked them up and down, studying them for injuries. Cormac was kneeling on the ground, Dane and Tristan stood next to him. All three of them wore expressions of surprise and then Cormac looked away from me, his brow furrowed as he studied Ethan's unmoving form.

I ran forward around the carcasses of the beasts and through their spilled entrails. I didn't even worry about where my feet fell. All I knew was that I had to get to Ethan.

Once I reached him, I fell to my knees near his head. I pushed a lock of hair away from his forehead and watched his chest for the rise and fall of breath. I let out a gasp of relief when I saw it move then sucked in a short breath of fear when I heard how his breath caught. He was struggling. *Aren't Fae supposed to be immortal? Shouldn't he be up and moving around?*

"What happened?" I asked.

Cormac lifted Ethan's tunic then removed the bundle of cloth they'd applied. Two large puncture wounds spanned his torso. One on his stomach, and one at the base of his ribcage. They didn't look like claw marks.

"The Sodalis bit him," Dane said, a growl in his voice.

"Why isn't he healing?" I asked.

"It was a female Sodalis," Cormac said.

"So?" I asked, desperation seeping into my voice.

"We've never seen a female here. They usually stay in the Under. They carry venom in their bite," Cormac said.

"He'll recover, though, right?" I'd seen the others heal from wounds that should have killed them. I'd healed from my own share of wounds that should have killed me.

"Do you see any healers here?" Tristan asked.

I glared at him. "He's recovered without a healer before."

"This is different," Cormac said.

"We have to help him," I said.

"We can take him to my palace," Tristan said. "It's close. The slide won't be as difficult on him. I'll call for a healer."

Cormac nodded, then slid his arms under Ethan and lifted him.

"You'll all need to be touching me," Tristan said. "Or you won't pass through the barrier."

Tristan wrapped his arm around my waist and pulled me close to him. I hardly felt the touch. I was too focused on watching Ethan's ragged breaths.

A moment later, everything went black.

Chapter Twenty-Nine

We walked through a gray stone corridor that passed in a blur. I kept my eyes locked on Cormac's back as he carried Ethan's unconscious form to wherever Tristan was taking us.

After all the things I'd heard about the Winter Prince, I didn't expect him to bring us to his home to treat a fallen Fae. This wasn't part of our bargain. He only agreed to help me and let them in to seal the tear. He didn't agree to help Ethan. I wondered how much of his reputation was earned or how much was speculation.

"In here," Tristan said, opening a large wood door.

Someone grabbed my upper arm. I turned to see Dane with a serious expression on his face. He pulled me back away from the room that Tristan, Cormac and Ethan went into. I stepped toward him. "What is it?"

"You have to know," he said, his lips turning down into a frown, "we don't have much experience with this venom."

My brow furrowed and I searched his eyes for some sign of hope. None of Dane's usual mischievous glimmer was present.

"If a healer can't get to him fast enough..."

"No," I said. "Don't finish that statement."

Tears welled up in my eyes, blurring my vision. I blinked and they streamed down my cheek. I pulled my arm away from Dane's grasp and shook my head. "That's not going to happen."

Wiping my eyes, I turned away from him and walked into the room.

Ethan was on a large canopy bed, the curtains tied open so we could see him better. Tristan nodded at me as he walked to the door. He paused and rested his hand on my shoulder. "I'm going to do what I can to save your friend. In the Winter Court, we take care of our own. And I know what Ethan means to you."

He gently squeezed my shoulder and left the room.

My head spun as I walked over to where Cormac sat on the edge of the bed next to Ethan. Tristan wasn't helping because of the deal I'd made him. He was helping because he thought I was a Winter Fae. Maybe it wasn't the worst thing to be from the Winter Court.

Cormac stood as I approached. "Dane and I have to go find the tear. We can't let this go on. If there are more female Sodalis that get through, it's going to mean a lot of dead Fae. We can't have that."

I nodded. "I know."

"Tristan is going to summon a healer," Cormac said.

I wasn't sure if he was trying to calm me or if he was trying to convince himself that he was doing the right thing.

"I'll stay with him," I said.

Cormac nodded.

Tristan returned to the room, a pile of towels in hand. He set them on the bed next to Ethan. "The healer is on her way, but it could be a few hours."

"He doesn't have a few hours," Dane said.

"I know, but it's the best I can do," Tristan said. "I've sent messengers. Someone might come sooner."

"Can't she just slide here?" I asked.

He shook his head. "Not all Fae can slide."

I frowned, then walked over to Ethan. He'd healed me and I'd even helped him heal Cormac. I looked up at the princes standing near the door. "I'll do it."

"No, Cassia," Cormac said. "That's more magic than you can wield."

"Winter Fae aren't known for healing abilities," Tristan said.

"She's not a Winter Fae," Dane said.

"She got through the barrier. That makes her a Winter Fae," Cormac said.

"I've seen her heal before," Cormac said.

"She's also got a talent for animals. She could be Autumn, like you." Dane lifted his chin toward Cormac.

"Which court I belong to isn't important," I said. "I have to try to heal Ethan. Even if it's just enough to keep him alive until a proper healer arrives."

"Let her try," Tristan said, shrugging his shoulders. "It can't hurt."

"I don't want you overdoing it," Cormac said. "You don't know your limits."

"We'll be fine here," I said. "Go seal that tear before any more of those monsters get through."

Cormac's jaw tensed. It looked like he was trying to decide if he should sit here with me or go do his job, but that didn't make sense. Still, I felt like I needed to give him an extra push. "Cormac, go. Do your job."

He nodded, then cleared his throat. "Let's go, Dane."

"Be careful, love," Dane said.

"I will," I said. "All of you be careful, too. Please. Come back to me in one piece."

Cormac and Dane left the room and Tristan hesitated at the door.

"You're going to help them, right?" I asked.

"Can you really heal?" he asked.

I nodded.

He lifted an eyebrow. "We're going to have a lot to talk about when we get back."

"That's fine, just go," I said.

Tristan walked to the doorway, then gave me a backward glance. "If you feel tired and dizzy, stop. That's the magic's way of telling you it's too much."

I nodded. "Thanks."

He left the room, closing the door behind him.

Finally alone, I let out a sigh of relief and turned my attention to Ethan. His face was pale and his full lips were purple.

My brow furrowed and my chest tightened at the sight of him. I had to help him. We couldn't afford to wait for a healer. I knew that I'd do whatever I could to help him. He'd saved me when I was wet and injured and alone on the road. It was my turn to save him.

I crawled onto the bed next to him and leaned down, kissing his forehead gently. "Ethan, you do not have my permission to go. I need you to help me with this. You hear me? I'm going to do what I can, but I could use your help here."

My throat tightened and I swallowed back the threatening tears. I needed to stay focused here, not emotional. Taking a deep breath, I lifted his shredded tunic and removed the crimson shreds of fabric from the wounds. The blood had soaked through and while it wasn't gushing as much, it was still wet. Usually, Ethan was able to stop the bleeding on his own. I'd learned that the Fae were generally fast healers, but those with healing abilities were even more efficient. The fact that the wounds were still seeping wasn't a good sign.

Grabbing some of the towels that Tristan had left on the bed, I pressed them to the wounds. Ethan flinched, probably reacting to the pain.

"Sorry," I said, trying to be more gentle. Maintaining the pressure on the punctures, I focused on sending whatever magic I had to Ethan. Nobody had taught me how to use magic formally, but I knew it was there. I'd worked next to Ethan once, the two of us channeling whatever it was that helped heal someone. Thinking back to that moment, I recalled how I'd felt that flicker of a spark deep inside me. It was different than the violent clawing I felt when I used the light. This felt like warmth. In a way, the magic reminded me of Ethan. It was gentle and kind and brought comfort.

Closing my eyes, I held onto that feeling while pressing my palms into the towels on top of the injuries. My shoulders felt warm, like I'd spent too much time in the sun, and that heat traveled down my arms into my hands and fingers. I didn't budge. I stayed where I was, sending whatever I could to Ethan. I needed him to come back to us. I needed him to recover from this. Like all of the princes, I couldn't imagine my life without him. Ethan was pure comfort and joy. While he was around, I felt safe and cared for. I knew he'd look out for me and would never say an unkind word.

A wave of dizziness washed through me and I opened my eyes to check the progress. I lifted the towels and frowned. The wounds looked like they were seeping less, but the skin wasn't closing yet. I glanced at the towels. They were covered in yellow goo. I wrinkled my nose and tossed the towels to the side, grabbing a fresh pair from the stack on the bed.

Taking another deep breath, I pressed my palms on top of the towels and focused on sending my magic to Ethan. With each ticking moment, I felt more and more lightheaded, but I pressed on, ignoring Tristan's words. I knew I wasn't there yet. And Ethan deserved to be saved.

I peeked at the injury again, and again discarded the towels, switching them out for clean ones. The punctures were still the same, less bleeding, but no sign of healing. Frowning, I added clean towels and resumed my position.

My chin dropped to my chest and I shook my head, startled at the sudden exhaustion that overtook me. Had I fallen asleep? I checked the towels again and there was less yellow goo, but still no skin healing.

Frustrated, I changed out the towels again and resumed the process. After a few more minutes, the world was spinning so badly, I couldn't sit up anymore. I knew I'd overdone it, but I didn't care. If I gave Ethan enough of a chance to stay alive until a real healer arrived, I did what I needed to do.

Exhausted, I lay down next to Ethan and closed my eyes.

Chapter Thirty

"**W**hat did you do?" Ethan's voice swirled around me, coming in and out of focus.

I felt heavy, and let my eyelids flutter before forcing them open. Ethan's beautiful face hovered inches above mine. He smiled at me and my heart leaped.

"You're alive." I breathed out the words like a prayer.

He ran his fingers through my hair and shook his head. "I thought I'd lost you."

"Me?" I asked. "You were the one that was bleeding to death." At the memory of his injury, I sat up, intending to check that he was healed. My head spun and I fell back onto the bed.

"Stay down," Ethan said. "I'm fine. I woke to find a healer sitting in the corner, but she didn't heal me. She said I was mended before she arrived."

My lips parted, but I didn't have any words. I was too happy to see him alive and well. I reached toward his face, tracing his pink lips with my fingertips. "I thought you were going to die."

"You shouldn't have used so much magic," he said. "I'm not worth the risk."

"Yes, you are." I stared into his clear blue eyes. How did

I make him understand how much he meant to me? I'd never felt a true connection to any human being before and here I was, feeling completely at ease with this Fae prince. It was as if we'd known each other our whole lives. Like we'd simply been apart for a few days but fell back into our old habits.

He leaned closer, slowly pausing with his lips above mine. I felt his warm breath on my skin and every inch of me felt like it was on fire. My breath hitched in anticipation and he pressed his lips against mine. His kiss was soft yet hungry and his lips moved with mine as if they were dancing. It was familiar and warm and maddening all at the same time.

His fingers wove through my hair, his hand cradling the back of my head, pressing me harder into him. I reached around him, digging my nails into the fabric of his ruined tunic and pulling him against me. His strong chest pressed against my breasts, making them ache for attention.

Ethan broke away for a moment, his shallow breaths matching my own. "Forgive me."

"For what?" I asked.

"That wasn't appropriate," he said. "There's just something about you that makes me lose control."

"Then lose it," I said. "I give you permission."

He hesitated for a second, then he pulled the bloody tunic up over his head and straddled me on the bed. I reached up to his muscled chest and dragged my fingers down his torso, stopping above the nearly healed puncture wounds on his stomach.

Ethan took my hands in his and guided them on top of the injuries. "You did this, you saved me. For that, I owe you more than I could ever give."

"I'd do it again," I said. "And I'd never ask anything of you."

He let go of my hands and a mischievous smile that would have looked natural on Dane appeared on his lips. "At least let me try to make it up to you."

I smiled back then pulled him down to me, running my fingers through his thick brown hair. "I won't try to stop you."

Ethan's fingers slid under my tunic and he carefully helped me pull it over my head. The spinning had eased and I could sit up now without falling over. Though, Ethan's touch was almost enough to make me feel just as lightheaded.

Gently, he traced his fingers down my shoulder, past my breast and down to my flat stomach. "You are a work of art."

I giggled and felt my cheeks heat. I knew I was pretty, but hearing it from someone you cared about was different than hearing it from strangers.

Ethan seemed to be drinking me in with his eyes then he lowered his head and kissed my stomach while his fingers loosened the ties on my trousers.

I lifted my hips to allow him to pull them off of me and when he slid them past my hips nervous flutters filled my stomach. I'd never been with a man and I wasn't sure what to expect. I knew sex wasn't viewed the same way here as it was in the human realm, but it was hard to let go of what I'd been raised with.

Ethan kissed the tops of my exposed thighs and gently pressed his lips on the raised hip bones. I sucked in a breath and held it as a shiver went down my spine.

He returned his attention to my mouth, his lips finding mine once again. He still had his trousers on, but I could feel the bulge of his erection pressed up against my thigh. Part of me wanted to feel the bare flesh against my own, but I wasn't in a hurry. His kisses were enough to leave me breathless.

Suddenly, his fingers were in between my legs and I gasped as he touched something that sent a shockwave of pleasure through me. My hips lifted in response and I pulled away from the kiss, eyes wide.

Ethan looked pleased with himself and touched me again, watching me gasp in pleasure. I felt wetness spread between my legs and moaned as Ethan continued to bring waves of pleasure with his fingers.

Slowly, he moved his hands to my hips and leaned in closer to me, as if waiting for me to give him a sign.

After a moment, I realized he was giving me the time to tell him to stop. I'd asked Dane to stop. I wasn't ready then. But now, with Ethan, everything felt right. I reached out to his belt and slowly removed the buckle.

He smiled and climbed off of me and stood next to the bed so he could remove his pants.

I thought the sight of a naked Fae male would shock me, but everything seemed so natural. Ethan settled back on top of me, pressing his erection at my entrance gently, teasing me.

Remembering what I'd heard about a woman's first time, I knew I needed a distraction. I laced my fingers around the back of Ethan's head, pulling his face to mine and kissed him fiercely.

He took that moment to enter me and I gasped into his mouth as a sharp pain flickered then eased. Ethan's mouth moved to my neck in a trail of soft kisses and the tension I'd felt melted away.

When we were finished, I curled up against Ethan, resting my head on his chest.

"Why didn't you tell me it was your first time?" he asked as he traced lazy circles with his fingertip on my shoulder.

"I didn't want you to change your mind," I said.

He kissed my forehead. "Thank you for that gift."

I laughed. "You know, I was practically naked the first time we met."

He smiled. "And you stole my heart that day."

"So did you," I said, leaning in to kiss him.

Suddenly, the door flew open and I screamed, grabbing the sheets to cover myself.

Dane, Cormac, and Tristan all walked into the room and the smell of dead Sodalis made me wrinkle my nose. All three of them were covered in blood. Some of it fresh. I wanted to ask what happened, but my mouth went dry. I never expected to have three Fae princes walk in on me with another Fae prince.

"Ethan?" Dane asked, laughing.

I felt my face heat and pulled the covers up over my head, scooting down under the blankets.

"The healer arrived in time?" Cormac asked, completely ignoring the scene in front of him as far as I could tell.

"Actually, it was Cassia. By the time the healer arrived, the wounds were already mending. Though, I think she over did it. She needs proper training," Ethan said. "Or she could end up hurting herself."

"Apparently she recovered rather quickly, too. We were only gone a day and a half," Tristan said. "Well done, both of you."

I ignored the implication of the comment and silently brooded under the blankets. "Please send them away," I whispered, hoping Ethan could hear me.

"We're leaving, Cassia," Dane said loudly. "Any place I can get a bath?"

"I'll send one to your room," Tristan said.

"We'll give you two some time," Cormac said. "Meet us downstairs in a half hour."

"Of course," Ethan said.

I bit down on my lower lip, holding my breath so I could hear the sound of the door closing behind them.

As soon as it sounded, Ethan tugged the covers off of me. "Are you alright?"

"I'm mortified," I said. "They all walked in here and saw us together. I didn't even get to explain anything to Dane."

Guilt tugged at my gut as I thought about how betrayed he must feel. And that didn't even begin to explain the feelings I had toward Cormac. Yet, I didn't regret my time with Ethan and I wouldn't trade it. How was it possible that I cared so deeply for all of them?

Ethan tucked a stray golden curl behind my ear. "Couldn't you tell? They were happy for us. Cormac and Dane are like brothers to me. We don't keep any secrets. I know how Dane feels about you and he knows how I feel about you. We aren't the jealous type."

"What about Cormac?" I asked.

"He's harder to read when it comes to females," Ethan frowned, "Angela broke his heart and he hasn't been the same since. I've only seen him take two females to bed in the last hundred years."

"Is it often that you share females with Dane?" I asked, feeling a surge of jealousy at the thought of any of them being with anyone besides me.

"We have, on occasion, but Cassia, never like this," he said. "You aren't a flight of fancy, there's something about you that makes me want to hold you and never let you go." He pulled me into an embrace.

I kissed his bicep. "I feel the same way about you, but I also feel that about Dane and Cormac."

"I understand," he said. "And if I had to share you with anyone, it would be them."

A gentle knock sounded on the door. I pulled the blankets up around me again, expecting to see more princes.

"Enter," Ethan called.

The door opened and several servants entered, carrying a large bathtub and buckets of water. Silently, they set the tub in the middle of the large room and poured bucket after bucket of steaming water into it.

After several minutes of pouring buckets in, the tub was full. One of the servants set two towels down on a nearby chair before taking her leave. Another servant draped two wash cloths over the side of the tub then set a bar of soap on top of them. A final maid laid out some folded clothing, setting it on the other chair in front of the room's fireplace. She curtseyed and exited the room, closing the door behind her.

The entire production was efficient and silent. The servants never spoke. I wondered why that was and hoped it was because they simply had nothing to say rather than required silence. There was so much I still needed to learn about this world.

Ethan hopped out of the bed then extended his hand. "Shall we?"

I took it with a giggle and followed him to the large tub. It was big enough for both of us, just barely. Ethan's legs wrapped around me as we soaked in the warm water. A sweet smelling oil rose with the steam from the water and I sank back against the edge of the tub, feeling absolute bliss.

Chapter Thirty-One

Tristan's castle was dripping in luxury. I hadn't noticed the details when we arrived, but now that I was walking through the hall with Ethan alive and well, I took the time to look around.

The floors were polished marble and the walls were lined with tapestries. Small tables holding busts and other sculptures were positioned between every door on the long hallway. The windows were clear or colored glass that allowed for so much natural light that the glowing candelabras weren't even needed this time of day.

We followed an elaborate winding staircase down to a grand room filled with pristine furniture and shelves that reached the ceiling filled with books. I could see other rooms outside of this one and I knew they were all just as opulent and lavish. Since we'd arrived right at the front doors and rushed inside, I wasn't even sure how large the building was. I wondered if I should ask for a tour.

Cormac, Dane, and Tristan were seated around a low round table, each in their own armchair. Across from them, a fire crackled and popped as flames danced behind the screen of the fireplace.

The princes looked the part again, clean and handsome. Each of them was dressed like Tristan in white tunics, gray trousers and black boots lined with fur. It was the same clothing that had been left for Ethan and it was clearly a much warmer ensemble than they were used to.

I was in a silver dress made of a thick fabric that reminded me of wool, but felt more delicate somehow. It was the first time I felt clean and properly clothed since arriving in Faerie and I appreciated it greatly. I smiled at Tristan, and curtseyed at him. "Thank you for your hospitality, my lord."

He stood and inclined his head. "My lady, won't you join us?"

Cormac and Dane stood, too.

I accepted Tristan's invitation and joined the others at one of the two empty chairs, Ethan settling next to me in the remaining seat.

"How did it go?" Ethan asked.

"The tear was right where we suspected it was on the southern border. We were able to dispatch a few remaining stragglers and seal it," Cormac said.

Ethan nodded. "That's good. I hope we won't see them again for a long time."

"Did you ever figure out why they were after me?" I asked.

The room was silent and I sensed something unsaid hanging between Cormac, Dane, and Tristan.

"What did you find?" Ethan said.

"We don't know for sure, but we have a theory," Cormac said.

"You say you healed him?" Tristan said, turning to me.

I nodded. "I did."

"And you accidentally entered the Winter Court?" he asked.

"Yes," I said. "You were there."

He pressed his lips together and furrowed his brow. It was almost like he was trying to work out a puzzle in his mind.

"What is your theory?" I asked, turning to Cormac.

"You've demonstrated skills from three of the four courts. You experienced seeing the future and you were able to enter the Winter Court, which are gifts only for those of Winter blood. Your ability to heal yourself and others is greater than that of a typical Fae; it aligns with the skills of those with Spring blood. You have a way with animals and your senses are keen which could indicate Autumn blood," Cormac paused. "And it's possible you're demonstrating some of the Summer Court's lust for life's pleasures."

I glanced at Dane. He'd been serious about that?

"Ethan would know more about that than me," Dane said.

"I don't think that matters right now," Ethan said. "Even having the skills of two courts would be unusual. Having the magic from three or four is unheard of. Only the queen herself can wield the magic of all four courts."

"True, it's not only impossible, it's also dangerous," Cormac said. "The creatures of the Under are attracted to magic. Untrained magic of more than one court in a single being would act like a beacon calling them in."

I shifted in my chair. If I had magic from multiple courts, what did that mean for me? I wasn't sure I liked the direction this was going. "What now? Monsters just keep coming after me for the rest of my life?"

Cormac shook his head. "Not after you learn to control it."

"Are you offering to teach me?" I asked.

"We all are," Dane said. "Even Tristan."

"Why?" I asked, looking over at the Winter Prince.

He leaned back in his chair. "I made a bargain with you. You teach me about humans, I help you. I can't exactly learn about humans if you're eaten by monsters. Besides, with you around and untrained, they'll keep coming into our lands. And I can't have that."

I took a deep breath. I had four princes offering to teach me how to use and control the magic I had inside me. Wasn't this what I always wanted? It should be a dream come true, but something didn't feel right. Then I remembered Angela's prediction. She said it was about the Sodalis, but now I knew better. "If I don't get this under control, bad things are going to happen, aren't they?"

"Maybe," Cormac said.

There was only one way to save myself and it turned out, there was so much more than my life in the balance. If I didn't learn how to tame the magic within, I was putting everyone at risk. I knew I had to do whatever I could to fix this. Cormac, Ethan, and Dane had saved my life. Now, it was my chance to save them. "When do we start?"

"Tomorrow," Dane said.

"There's only one Fae alive who knows how to fully channel all four kinds of magic," Cormac said. "We leave for the Royal Palace at dawn. We're going to see the queen."

Author Notes

Thank you for taking the time to read my book! I hope you enjoyed your time with Cassia and her princes!

Book Two is available for Pre-Order on Amazon

Want updates, news, and giveaways?
Join My Mailing List

Also by Dyan Chick
Magic Born, Dragon Mage Book 1
Magic Awakens, Dragon Mage Book 2
Magic Rising, Dragon Mage Book 3
Magic Returns, Dragon Mage Book 4
Fae Cursed: Legacy of Magic Book 1
Dark Fae: Legacy of Magic Book 2
Heir of Illaria: Book 1 of the Illaria Series
Oracle of Illaria: Book 2 of the Illaria Series
Battle of Illaria: Book 3 of the Illaria Series

Made in the USA
Middletown, DE
30 June 2020

11675179R00123